New Beginnings

By

Chaya Baila Weinfeld

The Judaica Press, Inc. ♦ 2000

Library of Congress Cataloging-in-Publication Data
New Beginnings
by Chaya Baila Weinfeld
p. cm.

ISBN 1-880582-46-5

[1. Adoption Fiction. 2. New York (N.Y.) Fiction.

3. Jews—United States Fiction.]   I. Title.
PZ7.W436368Ne   1999
[Fic]—dc21   CIP 99-33541

THE JUDAICA PRESS, INC.
123 Ditmas Avenue
Brooklyn, New York 11218
718-972-6200   800-972-6201
info@judaicapress.com
www.judaicapress.com

Manufactured in the United States of America

Table of Contents

Acknowledgements

The hardest part of writing this book was compiling the acknowledgements. *New Beginnings*, (like almost every novel) was begun with inspiration, written in frustration, and delivered with trepidation. The idea slowly took shape, with many false starts along the way.

Though writing is a solitary craft, I would be deluding myself, and the reader, by insinuating that the finished product is mine alone.

Here comes the easy part: So many friends have contributed, criticized, and cajoled me into writing this book. Without their support, *New Beginnings* would be yet another file on my computer, which I might peruse from time to time, wondering if—and when—it will ever be published.

Now for the difficult part: I'm afraid I'll inadvertently omit someone important, a loyal critic whose input made all the difference. Please forgive me if I do; your contribution toward *New Beginnings* shall live on in the book long after the reader has turned the last page.

So, here goes: To my dear parents, whose faultless advice and unerring vision have guided me, and propelled the book toward a "New Beginning." Mommy never failed to notice the contradictions and ambiguities between the lines; her red pen truly saved the book. Totty's effusive praise for every school assignment I ever composed gave me the encouragement to continue writing.

To the rest of my family: supportive in-laws, loyal siblings, and relatives, for their constant confidence, encouragement and support.

To my former students whose nudging (When is your book being published?), exerted subtle pressure upon me to "get my act together" and deliver the finished product to the publisher.

To my teachers and mentors throughout the years, who have given me guidance and nurtured the writing spark within. To Rebetzin Noa Flam of YSV and Mrs. Sue Rosen of the New School for encouraging me to "aim for the stars" and view each setback as a new challenge. To Mrs. Miriam Elias, my writing anchor for a decade, who has taken me under her wing as I stumbled through the ups and downs of launching a writing career.

To my friends, endowed with the knack of making me feel good even while good-naturedly tearing my book apart and putting it together again. To Debbie Maimon, Chanie Lipschutz, Rivky Pollack, Chaya Blima Twersky, the Schnitzlers, and all the others whose advice, comments and criticism helped form the raw material into a story.

To Bonnie Goldman, Barbara Weinblatt, Yehudis Friedman, Zisi Berkowitz, and the rest of the superb editorial staff at Judaica Press, for honing the raw material in these pages into a finished product and for being so supportive and pleasant to deal with. Their attitude made all the difference.

To the remarkable individuals I have met and interviewed throughout the years, whose haunting life stories of tragedy and triumph created the kernel of an idea in my mind, the catalyst for *New Beginnings*.

To my children for teaching me about the ingenuity, imagination, and innocence of childhood, and for filling my life with smudgy fingerprints, piles of laundry, happiness and love.

To my husband, for teaching me to believe in myself, for giving me the confidence to be both Mommy and writer. And for being such a devoted Totty when I was busy with my book.

My humble gratitude to the *Ribono Shel Olam* for

the treasure chest of blessings He has given us, and continues to do so everyday. May we be a source of *nachas* to Him always.

Forging Ahead

What if I told you that for the second time in my life, I was changing my address?

—Not just my address, but my city, state, and zip code as well.

Other things would also change...including my school, my family and friends—especially my sense of self.

As the train zoomed across the tracks and the flat, colorless landscape sped by my window, I found myself trying to contain the nervousness threatening to engulf me. I usually love to go places. But this was completely different. I was en route to a new beginning. And I couldn't even imagine where I was going or what my new life would be like!

Among my other possessions, I had stuck a *Tehillim* into my bag. The first few pages were torn out completely, many of the others were so worn that it was becoming difficult to read them. So I said the words aloud from memory, stopping between chapters to catch my breath.

After a few chapters, I squinted out of the grimy cubes that passed for windows, and the bright glare of the mid-afternoon sunshine squinted back. Was it winking at me, Rina Leah Berger and shining its rays upon my future? Would I finally be saying goodbye to the fog that had clouded my life for the past few years?

I opened my *Tehillim*, and turned to chapter 23:

"Mizmor l'Dovid, Hashem ro'ee lo echsor."

I read the English translation.

"Hashem is my Shepherd, I shall not want."

The words had a particular poignancy for me, and I must have gotten a little carried away and said it too loudly.

"What's gotten into that kid?" I turned my head, surprised. The voice was coming from a blonde teenage girl sprawled in the back of the train compartment, her legs dangling over her chair.

"Yeah, why can't she just pray herself outta here?" agreed her curly-haired friend, rolling her large black eyes.

I craned my neck for a better glimpse. The blonde one had her hair crimped wildly. Her friend loudly cracked an enormous piece of chewing gum.

I quickly stashed my *Tehillim* away. The last thing I wanted was to cause trouble before I had even arrived!

Anyway, I certainly wanted to avoid antagonizing these girls. They didn't look extremely tolerant. The train was almost empty, and these two were the only ones about my age.

That's all the social company I would have to look forward to on this trip. There was nothing else to see, save the green vinyl seats and commercial train carpet...

...and the endlessly bleak landscape racing past my window.

Across from my seat snoozed an elderly man wearing a rumpled gray suit and striped tie. On the adjoining seat, a prim gray-haired lady lifted the newspaper on her lap to glimpse the morning news.

She sensed my steady gaze and lifted her eyes disapprovingly. She seemed about to open her mouth and say something, but I averted my eyes quickly. A few minutes later, I discreetly peeked her way, but my embarrassed gaze met hers immediately.

"'Tain't proper to stare at people," she matter-of-factly remarked.

"I didn't stare," I responded, perhaps a little too defensively.

"Don't you know better than to answer your

elders back? I'm about old enough to be your grandma, young miss."

"I'm sure glad you're not!" I mumbled under my breath.

Her remark awoke her husband, who rubbed his mustache in a tired sort of way and looked up.

"Alan, do you hear how these teenagers talk today?" she said to her husband, pointing long wrinkled fingers in my direction. "I declare, she reminds me of your sister Emily. Always staring and poking her nose where she isn't wanted."

"Now, now," her husband tried to mollify. "Emily isn't all that rude. Remember the silverware she bought us for our golden wedding anniversary?"

"Yes, and insisted that we use it every night. Such nerve! What business is it of hers if we want to save it for special occasions?" she ended, puffing in indignation. They had completely forgotten about me, or would have forgotten, if not for my big mouth.

"Mom used to set out the silverware for dinner every night," I cut in proudly. The instant the words had left my tongue I wished I could have pulled them back with a lasso. The couple looked up, startled.

Now, don't get me wrong. I'm not immature, or anything of the sort. Actually, I'm quite wise for my twelve-and-a-half years and Minnie Mouse height. (4'10" the last time I measured.) The only thing about me I wish could shrink is my mouth. I usually think about my words—after they are said—and the thoughts are anything but complimentary.

"Just who is this mother of yours who lets a little thing like you travel alone?"

"Harriet, leave the girl alone. It's none of your business."

"Why, of course it is my business. I wouldn't be surprised if this little know-it-all is one of them runaways."

I didn't wait to hear the rest.

I threw my faded travel bag over my shoulder, and stomped out of the car, leaving the teenaged girls staring, open mouthed, at my receding back. I squared my shoulders stiffly and continued, as the bag bounced on my shoulder.

Compared to the train car I had just left, this one seemed quite full. Most of the seats were taken by what appeared to be first-class travelers, dressed in staid apparel, speaking in measured tones. I glanced down at my plaid woolen skirt with distaste. That, and the frayed white blouse and navy sweater, were about the finest things I owned. The rest of my belongings were crammed into a battered suitcase, stored in a luggage rack in the previous car.

Suddenly, the loudspeaker system came to life, startling me.

"Attention all passengers. We are now serving lunch. All passengers, please be seated. Lunch is now being served."

The nasal voice crackled over the loudspeaker, and several passengers folded their newspapers, waiting expectantly for their meal.

As the kitchen staff began to wheel the trays, the aroma wafted in from the kitchen, tickling my nose. My stomach complained with a grumble, and a glance at my battered plastic watch confirmed what I had felt. I hadn't had a thing to eat all morning.

"Have a seat young lady, will you? There's plenty of room, and you don't want to miss lunch." The uniformed attendant pointed to a seat near the end of the compartment.

I looked at her appraisingly. She was a large woman, with severe features and a no-nonsense attitude. Her name tag read "Martha". Would she be willing to help?

"Uh....I wanted to ask....maybe....I think my uncle ordered a kosher meal for me."

She paused and looked at me.

"If you'll just tell me your name, I'll go back and check in an instant...."

"Rina. Rina Berger."

I watched her heels click on the fraying carpet as she left. Within minutes, Martha returned, shaking her head.

"I'm really sorry, dear, but there is no kosher meal ordered for a Rina Berger."

"But I'm sure—"

"There is no kosher meal for you in our kitchen,"

she repeated firmly.

"Nothing? Nothing for Berger at all?" I asked, hungry and desperate.

"Look here," she was visibly annoyed.

"I said there was nothing for Rina. There is a kosher meal for Berger, but not for a Rina Berger."

My cheeks suddenly grew hot. True, Aunt Shifra had always insisted on calling me Leah—my second name. She never did like the name Rina, perhaps because of my fixation with it. She couldn't understand why I didn't use Leah—the name of my mother's mother, who had passed away before I was born. Because I never knew my bubby, the name held no memories for me. That bothered Aunt Shifra to no end. And if it bothered my aunt, it bothered my uncle. He insisted I use the name Leah.

Uncle Michael was like that, tending to assert his authority over little matters that didn't really mean much, except as a bargaining tool. His constant question, "Leah, did you do your homework yet?" would grate on my nerves.

Martha watched my changing facial expression with a sardonic smile.

"Now you're going to tell me your name is Leah, is that right?"

"But it is!" My voice came out a trifle louder then I meant it to, because, once again, I became the center of attention as all the passengers turned to look at me.

"Don't take me for a fool. Just because you forgot to order a kosher meal doesn't give you the right to take away someone's por—" I couldn't help but interrupt her.

"I'm not taking away anyone's portion! My name *is* Leah. But it's also Rina! I can see you don't believe me, anyway."

"Who's not believing whom?" A cheerful voice boomed from the doorway. It came from a roly poly man, with a round reddish face. He a porter's cap and he looked old. Fluffy gray down covered his wrinkled forehead, and he had an oddly pointed a reddish nose.

"Tell Josh about the little trouble here, and whoosh!" he pulled a white kerchief from his overall pocket and folded it flat. "See if Josh can't fix it straight."

Martha seemed irritated by Josh's appearance. "Save your fixing for some other time, Josh. This isn't of any importance to you at all!"

"Are you kidding? Everything that happens on this train is important to me. This is my train!" His bluster was transparent, and spoken with such mock swagger that the other passengers were trying to hide their smiles.

And before I could control my slippery tongue, it started to control the situation.

"Josh, I....uh....have a little problem here," I said, pointing to Martha. "She says I didn't order a kosher meal, but I did."

"Hmm.... Martha says you didn't, and you say you did. That is a major problem. After all, we can't let this redhead go hungry, can we?"

He gestured to me and led the way to the kitchen.

It was the first time in my life that someone had called me a redhead—to my face—and I wasn't even angry. For in Josh I instinctively felt I had a friend.

And for me, friends weren't easy to come by.

And I didn't think the situation would improve one bit in my new life.

As the train rolled further away from the only hometown I'd ever known, I felt as if I was leaving my childhood—as well as my identity—back home.

I stood in the back of the cramped dining car waiting for Josh, as dining car workers ran in and out carrying supplies and I suddenly dreaded returning to my seat.

"Let me stay here and eat, Josh. Pleeeaassse...."

"Well, it's not really allowed, except for staff."

"I just can't face that woman...."

"Oh, you mean Martha. Don't you worry about her. Her bark is worse than her bite," he winked at me.

I perched on a stainless steel bar stool, my legs swinging freely. In my lap was the kosher food plate which Josh had procured for me. I quickly peeled away the covering, exposing an overwhipped mound of mashed potatoes and a slightly wrinkled flounder smothered in tomato sauce. Some steamed broccoli was piled in the third compartment of the container. The rest of the tray held an apple and a can of soda. I hadn't had any soda in a long time.... Uncle Michael didn't believe in soft drinks for young, growing girls. "Why would you want to drink such junk?" he asked, whenever we had begged him for a Rosh Chodesh treat. "It's loaded with artificial sweeteners and chemicals."

Now I didn't care. I was grateful Uncle Michael had managed to get this kosher meal specially ordered for me. This is one meal I'm going to enjoy, I thought. I did have a hard time opening the plastic bag containing the utensils, finally ripping it with my teeth. Though the menu left much to be desired, I was too hungry to care. I self-consciously made a bracha, as Josh curiously watched me. I wondered if he realized what I was saying, but I didn't bother explaining. The food was reasonably warm and I was starved, so I pitched in with relish.

Another dining car worker walked in and out of the room getting supplies and Josh busied himself around the kitchen, stopping occasionally to smile at my appetite.

"So your 'Daddy' forgot to say your name was Rina, eh?"

"My uncle, not my Daddy—and he didn't forget. He doesn't like the name Rina, which is the only way I like to be called."

"Rina," he sounded it out. "It sounds right to me, though I think Leah is more your style."

"Leah? It sounds so old fashioned."

"Old fashioned and royal. Like a princess. But you don't look much like a princess to me," he added as an afterthought. "More like the classroom trouble maker, I'd say."

I giggled. How right he was! Only my trouble-making days, it seemed, were far from over. Now other people were making the trouble for me.

"Well, you're not the only one, Rina," Josh genially added. "I say, there's nothing like a little trouble to get a railroad station zapping! Nothing like it!"

"Watch this!" Josh pulled a microphone out of his pocket and began speaking.

"Attention all passengers, attention passengers! This is Josh your conductor speaking. We're sorry for the inconvenience, but this train will be arriving at the station about two minutes late. I repeat—"

He repeated his message twice, and was about to repeat it a third time, when....

"What do you think you're doing?" the microphone dropped to the floor, as Josh swung to face the manager, a picture of wrath.

"Who gave you permission to make such a ridiculous statement? Two minutes late, indeed!"

"I just thought it was better to alert passengers in case we were late!"

I winked at Josh and smirked. The manager snorted.

"Hmph! I don't know where you find the energy for these shenanigans!"

"Come on! After all I've done for the railroad all these yea—"

"Cut it out, Josh. How many times a day do I have to be reminded that you've been with us for fifteen years and have lifted more suitcases than I've seen passengers?!"

"Or that I've always been reliable, punctual and trustworthy?"

"Yeah, yeah, go ahead. Give yourself another few pats on the back."

By now, I was giggling so loud that my breath escaped in short gasps. There weren't too many more like Josh, of that I was sure....

Within the hour Josh made another announcement: "Last stop, all passengers out!"

The train seemed to let out a long loud sigh as it slowed to a steady stop, the engines vibrating from the strain. The doors swung open noiselessly and instantly, the passengers waiting by the doors began to disembark, quickly pulling their luggage down the train's stairs and hurrying down the train platform.

I clutched my bag, bewildered. Uncle Michael had given me the number of a taxi, as well as exact instructions on how to get to the airport. There I was supposed to board a nonstop flight for New York. Of course, he and Aunt Shifra had offered to accompany me until the plane, but I would hear nothing of it.

"If I'm old enough to move away all alone, I'm old enough to get there by myself," I said, emphasizing every hurtful syllable. Boy, were they offended.

Actually, there were some complications with my flight. The Steins, my "new parents," were supposed to come and pick me up, but at the last minute, it didn't work out. I had a feeling Uncle Michael and Aunt Shifra asked them not to come. I don't know why but I don't think there is any "love lost" between them. Now, if I could only locate my baggage! Most of the other passengers were still milling about the large, disorderly platform. I recognized the elderly couple who had been so rude. They were arguing with an indignant porter, and I could only catch a few words which sounded like "doesn't deserve a tip."

I began to get nervous, looking around frantically, trying to locate a helpful face—anyone—who was here to help.

Hashem heard my unspoken prayers, and sent a friendly voice, right at my elbow.

"Oh, if it isn't my redheaded friend. I've been lookin' for you all over! Do you want the train to leave the station with your suitcase?" It was Josh. And in his hand he clutched the handle of my familiar ragged suitcase. I was so happy to see him!

"Oh, Josh. Thank you! Thank you! You've made my trip so much better! Thank you so much!" I blabbered.

"Don't mention it, Rina," Josh said, a big smile on his face.

"You're an extraordinary little girl traveling all by yourself so bravely! Whatever name you have!"

"Josh!" Suddenly I knew I had to tell him. "I'm going to live...with...somebody I've never met. I'm really scared."

"Don't worry, you'll be all right. Just say a few of those prayers you've been mumbling, and whoosh!—everything will be all right."

So he had noticed, after all.

Josh set my suitcase down carefully, gave me a last wide smile and before I could say anything he disappeared with a wave into the smoky engine compartment. I stood rooted to my spot as the train's engine whistled and the cars slowly rolled out of sight.

I felt more alone than before I had boarded the train. It's harder to have friends and lose them than not to have any in the first place, I discovered, much to my chagrin.

Now what?

I need a cab, I thought. I looked at my watch. Twelve fifteen my time. My flight to New York was supposed to leave at one thirty, and according to

Uncle Michael, the airport was a fifteen minute ride from the train station.

I walked over to the nearest pay phone, lugging my suitcase and pulled out the paper Uncle Michael had given me with the cab company's phone number.

"It'll be at least a ten minute wait," said the dispatcher.

I resigned myself to waiting, but without realizing it, I had begun to pace the platform nervously. The throngs of people from the train had all gone, and now the platform and station were nearly deserted. It looked spooky in the artificial lighting; down here, I couldn't tell whether it was night or day.

Worst of all, it seemed as if almost everyone had a best friend or relative to meet them at the station. Only a solitary girl (me!) had nobody to greet her as she walked out into the great wide world.

And believe it or not, nobody seemed to care. I wouldn't have minded if someone—anyone—even a policeman would have stopped me and said, "Hey, little girl, are you waiting for someone?" but the young man at the ticket booth didn't even look up as I walked past, so engrossed was he in a phone conversation. The security guard in the corner was drinking a coke and couldn't care less about seeing me alone in the station.

I was starting to feel really depressed, so I returned to the public phone. I needed to talk to a familiar voice—someone back home.

"0-6-1-2–3-2-6–1-2-3-3."

After an agonizingly long wait, a tired voice came on the line.

"Operator, can I help you?"

"Yes. I would like to make a collect call."

"Your name?"

"Rina."

"Hold on."

Rrring....rrring....rrring....rrring....The phone at their end rang seven times, and the operator was about to give up, when someone answered.

I knew it was Shira, by the way she said, "Uh, hello?"

"This is the operator speaking. You have a collect call from—"

"Rina," I eagerly put in.

"Collect call from Rina. Will you accept the charges?"

"Yes, I mean, nobody is really home now—"

The operator hung up, and we were connected.

"Hi, Shira, it's me...it's Rina!"

"Where on earth are you calling from? Did you arrive already?"

"I'm still at the train station, waiting for my taxi. Where's everyone?"

"Daddy isn't home right now. He's out at a meeting with his boss."

"And your mother?"

"She's busy with the babies."

That figured. Since the birth of the twins there was little else Aunt Shifra could find time for. Every minute of every waking hour was occupied with the babies. The other kids had to fend for themselves as best as they could.

"Did you hear from Malky yet?"

"Of course not. She's probably still on the airplane."

At the mention of my sister, tears welled up in my eyes. Malky was the only real family member I had left, the only person in my life that I loved.

And now she was en route to our Tante Rachel in London, while I was forced to go live with strangers—people I had never even met, people who had no idea what I was like.

Some of my loneliness must have drifted over the lines, for Shira sounded concerned.

"Rina, are you all right?"

"I'm fine, really. Just a little homesick," I said.

Actually, it wasn't true. Overworked, underpaid Uncle Michael and exhausted Aunt Shifra and their lively brood would not be terribly missed.

But I didn't say it out loud. Though a half year older than I am, Shira wouldn't understand. There were many things about me that she didn't understand. Shira was all black and white, pragmatic and no-nonsense, while my personality was filled with fuzzy shades of gray. In addition, these were her parents, who had loved her unconditionally all her life, while I was practically an orphan.

I sighed and realized that Shira could not offer me what I needed. Besides, it was probably going to be an expensive call and Uncle Michael would be angry.

"Okay, Shira, gotta go."

"Okay, Rina. *B'hatzlacha*! I really hope that your new life in New York is great!" she added, with uncharacteristic warmth.

"Bye!"

I put down the receiver.

Of all my Kagan cousins (there were eight of them in all), Shira wasn't the worst. Now that Malky and I would no longer be sharing a room with her and two of her sisters, I was able to actually miss her.

I walked up the stairs of the underground station, holding on to the grimy railing. As I blinked in the unaccustomed daylight and began to get my bearings, the blue-and-white taxi arrived, honking noisily.

I gingerly put my suitcase into the trunk and told the driver which airline I was taking. Then I settled back on the vinyl cushions to indulge in my favorite pastime, thinking....

As I relaxed, my thoughts (naturally) turned to Malky. I closed my eyes and tried to concentrate on her expression when she was mad, on the way she tried to hold back tears, her lower lip trembling, or the way her face lit up when she rewarded you with a rare smile.

Malky was eighteen months younger than I, and we were inseparable. Too bad the London cousins only had room for one of us, though they wished they could take us both. Aunt Shifra had decided it would be too much for her brother and sister-in-law. And too bad it was Malky who was going and not me.

But Malky deserved it. I knew I should stop being so selfish. At least one of us would be happy! And I was stronger. I could take planes, trains, buses and taxis all by myself to meet some unknown aunt and uncle in some city that I had never seen.

The taxi driver zoomed down avenues, sped around curbs, trying to beat the traffic. Still, we were stuck behind a tractor-trailer for ten agonizing minutes. Finally, Mr. Taxicab tried a daring (probably illegal) move, weaving into traffic and coming out ahead of the snarl. My heart in my mouth, I searched for my seat belt and avoided looking at my watch; it was make it or miss it, and missing the flight would be disastrous!

The airport looked large and quite forbidding (not that I really knew anything about airports...).

The cabbie, wearing a weather-beaten cap and dangling a cigarette in his hand, insisted on escorting me to the ticket counter.

"Just to make sure you catch your flight," he

said, grinning as he demanded a hefty fee.

I took some money from the sealed envelope which Uncle Michael had prepared. Then the cabbie disappeared, and I stood before the counter with my single suitcase, feeling exceedingly small.

"Can I see your ticket, please?" The man at the counter looked at my ticket carefully, as I waited on pins and needles.

Finally he was satisfied that everything was in order and he handed me a boarding pass. "Hurry up, your plane is leaving in ten minutes. You've got to run!"

"Traveling by yourself today?" an airport attendant inquired as I raced up the escalator, too impatient to wait until it got to the top. I nodded impatiently. Didn't she see that I was in a rush?

They were closing the doors just as I raced up the ramp. I barely made it to my seat as the "fasten seat-belt" sign lit up. My breathing was rapid and shallow from the frenzied rush, prompting a pretty stewardess to ask, "Honey, are you all right?"

"Yes, I'm fine, thank you," I said, smiling back at her, trying to catch my breath. But she had already disappeared down the aisle.

The pilot announced that the flight to New York would only take three hours, and I was zonked.

I settled back in my seat, and dozed off. The ride was a little bumpy and we ran into some "turbulence," so I kept on waking up, terrified that we were about to crash. In this semi-conscious state images of my last week with my sister rose in my mind. I remembered the goodbye cake Shira had baked, the whispered conferences in our shared bedroom, the farewell cards we left for our aunt and uncle. But I avoided thinking of the most painful memory of all—the day it was decided that we couldn't live at the Kagans anymore.

Reflections

I huddled in my seat near the window, trying to remain inconspicuous. Nearby, a garishly-dressed middle aged businessman sat impatiently, rifling through his business papers. A few rows behind me, a baby whimpered. "Shh..." said her mother gently, and then began to sing.

"Hush little baby, don't you cry, Mom's gonna sing you a lullaby."

Her voice was thin and musical, and I found myself drawn to the simple drama of a mother singing to her child. And I felt a lump form in my throat. When was the last time my mother had sung to me?

Then the memories came, tumbling over one

another in their eagerness. Almost without meaning to, my mind reverted to that dreaded scene, the one that helped decide my destiny.

It was a Wednesday afternoon, after school. I sat in the large bedroom Malky, and I shared with the three Kagan sisters, trying to finish my math homework. I had absolutely no patience for formulas, and the circumference of the circle was to me the most boring thing in the world.

There was a hesitant knock on my door.

"Come in," I called, not looking up from my math book.

"Leah, can you come with me into the study? I have some news." That was my uncle, home from work, (already?)

Uncle Michael rarely spoke to me so directly. Curiosity piqued, I followed him. But there was an uneasy feeling in the pit of my stomach.

As I followed him into his tiny study, really an alcove off the kitchen, I was surprised to find Aunt Shifra, Shira and Malky already there, sitting on the couch. Malky was as bewildered as I was, though Shira looked like she knew something we didn't. I felt a surge of irritation as I avoided Shira's gaze. Why did she always have to poke her nose into everything?

Uncle Michael cleared his throat and then looked straight at me.

"Since you've moved in with us, ahem, (he looked

really uncomfortable) a few years ago, Shifra and I have tried to do our duty towards her sister's children, to be the kind of substitute parents she would have wanted us to be. (Ha? was he serious?). We've tried our best, but apparently, the best wasn't good enough."

Aunt Shifra, sitting on the couch, looked kind of pale. She wasn't sleeping well these days, because of the twins. But I don't think that's what was bothering her right now. Malky and I were her sister's children, and I knew she had pledged to care for us. I wondered what was going through her mind.

To his credit, Uncle Michael took the blame for himself and his wife. But he didn't fool anyone. Malky and I knew that we were mostly to blame.

Our aunt and uncle looked at us expectantly, waiting for us to say something. When nothing was forthcoming, Uncle Michael continued.

"We've had to make other arrangements for you girls," he continued, uncomfortably. "I...uh...Shifra and I have spoken to your Uncle David and Aunt Rachel in London. Though they'd love to have you both, they also have a large family, and we've decided and they've agreed that the only solution was to split up you girls. Since one of their daughters is about Malky's age, we've decided that Malky should be the one to go to London. I'm really very sorry to have to split you girls up. It's the last thing your Aunt Shifra and I wanted to do...I know how attached you are to each other."

I let out a long breath. So this is what it had come to! We were to be divided, like cute little puppies in a litter, doled out here and there. I was furious, but my pain was greater than my anger. And so I remained silent, not looking at anyone, clutching my knuckles, feeling my face turn colors, first red and then white.

"As for you, Leah, Shifra and I have discussed it at length. We feel that New York would be the best place for you, at least temporarily."

New York? The Big Apple? That noisy, big city? Where would I live?

Now Aunt Shifra spoke up, her voice betraying her emotion. "...And you'll be staying with other relatives of yours. They have one son, but he's married. They live in a beautiful suburb in New York, and they are quite well-off. They are also very educated—she has a Ph.D. in education, I believe. The Steins are eager to have you live with them, but we made it quite clear that it was only for a year or so, until better arrangements could be found. We feel that you sisters should stay together."

"Oh, sure. If you feel that way, why aren't you making more of an effort to keep us?" I wanted to say, but said nothing. Inside though, I couldn't help wondering.

Wealthy relatives in New York? If I had an aunt and uncle in New York, how come I'd never heard of them before? Then again, Mommy had come from Russia as a very young child, with her mother, sister and brother. Her mother, my bubby, passed away before I was born, so I never knew her at all. Mommy's father had passed away in Russia.

There were no relatives on my father's side, at least not any I knew. Or maybe there were. Mommy did not usually like to talk about her relatives, and we hadn't done much talking about things other than her illness in the year before she died. I vaguely remembered something, about rich relatives who wanted to come and take care of us when she was sick, but she refused. I wondered if it was them.

While all these thoughts were racing about in my head, I struggled to maintain a calm facade. Malky inched over to me, putting my hand in hers, perhaps so both of us could be strengthened. I ignored her squeeze, Shira's prying stare, my uncle's penetrating gaze. The die was cast. All I wanted was to be alone.

I looked straight ahead, not uttering a sound, trying hard not to cry. Malky's eyes, however, filled with tears.

Why, oh, why did my mother have to die? Why did my life seem to always take the most unexpected and worst turns? Now I would be separated from the only person in the world who I cared about!

"I really can't say how sorry I am," Uncle Michael said again, trying to help the situation.

"But maybe you'll be happier than you've been for the past few weeks!" he said, trying to find something good to say.

Poor Uncle Michael! Our relationship had been doomed to failure from the start. Even when Mother was alive she had never really gotten along with him well, referring to him only as her "brother-in-law."

For an instant, I felt the tiniest bit of sympathy for my uncle. It wasn't completely his fault that I had to be sent away.

"Well, I guess there is nothing we can do but make the best of it," I offered, trying to assume a cheerful facade, fooling no one.

"I'm sure you'll like it, Rina," Malky spoke up. But tears rolled down her cheeks. My heart ached for her, going off alone—she would suffer from our separation more than I. Since our mother had gotten sick almost three years ago, and even before— when our parents had divorced and Daddy had moved to Australia and remarried—we had always leaned on each other.

Life was idyllic when it had been just the three of us, Mommy, Malky and I. We went to school while Mommy taught in a local nursery school, and spent the rest of her time cooking and doing laundry, tending to our needs. We never went anywhere, even for the *Yomim Tovim*. The only exception was the *seder*, when we were invited to Uncle Michael and Aunt Shifra's place. Otherwise, we fended for ourselves quite well, thank you.

Life was a bowl of cherries, at least until that fateful phone call that transformed our simple, cheerful home into a nightmare.

The memories of that day are forever seared in my memory.

Mommy and I were in the kitchen, companionably cooking supper. We enjoyed working together, mother and daughter, more like two best friends. Though I was only ten years old, I was surprisingly proficient at peeling potatoes.

Malky was curled up on the couch, in the midst of reading a book, as usual. She had read through most of the children's books in our small-town library; the librarian jokingly told her that it was time to move on.

The kitchen clock ticked away, and the yellow refrigerator hummed as we clattered about. The sweet potatoes bubbled on the stove, and Mommy was about to check the chicken in the oven when the phone rang.

I raced to answer it, but Mommy was quicker than I, and intercepted the receiver. She must have been expecting the call, because she normally wasn't one to rush to answer phones. In fact, Mommy frequently turned on the answering machine, especially when the three of us ate supper. It was our own "family time" as Malky dubbed it, and phone calls, Mommy always said, could wait until we were done.

"Hello?" said Mommy.

Then she was silent for a long time. I couldn't tell who was speaking to her, because all she said, in a low voice, every time there was a lull in the conversation, was a serious "yes." There was something about the way she spoke that scared me. I looked at her face carefully, and suddenly realized that something was extremely wrong. "Malky?" I called out, walking into the next room.

"Mm....Hmm...." was all I got as a response. When Malky was reading, she was completely absorbed, to the exclusion of anything else.

Mommy was whispering now, talking to the mysterious "someone," her back to the door. I had a sinking feeling in the pit of my stomach; something was going on, and I was sure it wasn't at all pleasant.

I paced the living room floor, waiting for her to hang up. As I did, my mind filtered back to the painful time, four years before, when my parents had divorced. I was much younger then, but I vividly remember the hushed arguments and phone calls, the whisperings, the flurry of activity...now Mommy had put down the phone, and walked into the room.

"Girls," she said, "That was the doctor I went to last week for a blood test. I'm going to need a biopsy."

The blood drained from my face. I didn't know what "biopsy'" meant, but I could tell it wasn't a good thing. Malky looked at the terror mirrored in my eyes, and began to cry.

Mother went to calm her, sitting next to her on the couch and patting her back.

"Sh...don't worry," she said. "Hashem will take care of us. We'll be fine."

And for a while, we were. The three of us sheltered and protected each other through the endless doctors visits. Malky and I refused to be sent away, and we remained at home with Mommy while she recuperated from the grueling rounds of chemotherapy and radiation treatments. She grew progressively weaker and soon even simple tasks became difficult. Malky and I watched our precious mother become a shadow of her former self, and we were helpless to do anything about it. Our days passed in a daze of hopelessness and wrenching agony; nights were sleepless and endless, as Malky and I huddled together, waiting for sunrise. Aunt Shifra begged us to stay with her but we refused. We wanted to stay together.

Six months was all it took.

During those difficult months, I felt more alone than ever. Daddy was a stranger to us, and though he called sometimes, and offered to have us come stay with him, we felt uncomfortable joining his new wife and her two children from a previous marriage. Plus Mommy was absolutely opposed. So as Mommy became weaker and was hospitalized more often than not, we needed someone to care for us, wash our clothes and make sure our homework was done.

Not really having a choice, we moved in with our uncle and aunt—our only relatives—who lived in the same town as us, but from the start it was not the best arrangement. Uncle Michael worked hard but never had enough money to feed his brood, and Aunt Shifra was overwhelmed by the demands of her growing family. When Mother was still alive, we behaved, for her sake, but after she suddenly passed away—one afternoon while we were in school—all the remaining sunshine appeared to have been squeezed out of our lives.

I remembered that day, a Monday, because it was the day Malky and I were supposed to visit Mommy. On our last visit, the day before, Mommy's wan face and her trembling hands, all skin and bones, scared us. I didn't recognize my own mother.

"Rina, Malky," Mommy whispered, hugging us with tears in her eyes. We hugged her back gingerly, afraid to squeeze too tight. She looked so frail, so fragile, as if a breath of wind would blow her away.

We perched on the edge of her bed and told her a bit about school.

"That's it, girls. The visit's over," the stern nurse shooed us out of the room. We blew Mommy a kiss and waved to her, and that was our last glimpse of her, waving back with all her strength. She saved every bit of strength for us, her girls, all she had left in the world.

I eagerly looked forward to our visit all day during school though I dreaded seeing how Mommy seemed to become more shrunken each week.

I was spared the agony. An agony far greater, far deeper and far more raw was to come.

As I walked home from school, and was near Aunt Shifra's house the sight of my cousin Shira, running down the stairs to me, disheveled and pale, unnerved me. I had a fleeting intuition of bad news, but quickly banished it from my mind. "It's okay, Mommy's fine," I kept repeating to myself.

"What happened?" Malky asked, coming up behind me, frightened to see Shira running toward us.

"Oh, Rina, Malky," Shira sobbed. "It's terrible. They just called from the hospital."

"Shira!" Aunt Shifra's annoyed voice resounded from the house. "Come in quickly!"

Shira turned and ran, Malky and I following on her heels. Aunt Shifra sounded annoyed, probably because she didn't want to be the one to tell us.

She lifted her red-rimmed eyes to us, and we saw she had been crying. That meant bad news.

"What happened?" I asked, breathlessly. "Is it about Mommy?"

Aunt Shifra nodded.

"Is it something awfully bad?" I asked, stalling for time.

Another nod.

I couldn't bring myself to ask the next question,

but I didn't need to. The phone rang, and as I stood nearby, I picked it up.

"Hello?"

"Mrs. Kagan?" said an unfamiliar voice. "This is Brenda's nurse calling."

Filled with dread, I passed the phone to Aunt Shifra.

I stood near her, my heart beating rapidly. Suddenly, I heard her drop the phone and say,

"It's over. *Boruch Dayan Emes.*"

I let out a shriek and raced to my room. Malky followed, sobbing hysterically. Once there, I waited for the tears to come.

They never came.

My heart was broken, but all that emerged was a soundless cry, a cry that pierced the heavens.

I sat, stunned, for a long time, reeling from the blow. At first I didn't even notice Malky sitting beside me, clutching my hand.

Finally, after what seemed an eternity, Malky sniffed, breaking my reverie.

"We're all alone in the world now, Malky," I said to her.

We sat *shiva*, Aunt Shifra, Malky and I. Malky and I didn't have to sit *shiva* since we weren't twelve, but we wanted to. Uncle David, my mother's brother, sat *shiva* in London. All my friends and neighbors in the small town came to sit with us and, in endless succession, related stories about

Mommy. I listened carefully, absorbing it all, living moment by moment. I was numb, frozen, in shock, not allowing myself to think of the future.

Seven days was all it took. *Shiva* was over. Time to move on, with the rest of my motherless life stretching out endlessly before me. Instinctively, I knew the pain wouldn't always be as strong, and eventually would fade into a dull ache.

Daddy called from Australia, half-heartedly offering us a home, knowing how strongly Mother had felt about not allowing us to live with his new family. He did not press the issue. Mother had made Aunt Shifra promise that we would not go to Australia.

Our stay at our Kagan cousins didn't work out that well. Malky and I were not in the best of spirits, and we didn't try to get along with their family.

In hindsight, Malky and I were two angry, confused orphans left alone in the world, not quite nine and ten years old. At our aunt and uncle's home, we were tolerated, even treated kindly, but it definitely was not where we belonged.

Aunt Shifra smiled at us, two pathetic figures shuffling through the front door after school, giving us a peck on the cheek and asking about our day. We answered dutifully, ate our snack, and escaped upstairs to our room as soon as we could. There we would unwind, read and talk about our day, and relive memories of more carefree days. When we had lost our mother, we felt as if we had lost our childhood as well. And we felt wary of getting close to anyone ever again.

Aunt Shifra was also bereaved, having lost her only sister. The two had been especially close. Their only brother lived in London, and they had no other family. There was a close relative who lived somewhere in Europe, who used to write and call Mommy but didn't call Aunt Shifra or us after Mommy passed away. I didn't know too much about them, and I wasn't really interested. Had I known what the future would bring...but of course, I had no clue. How could I?

Shira shared the large and now crowded room with us, but I'm sure she felt somewhat unwanted—an intruder in the room that used to be shared by her and her sisters, Chaya and Kayla. I didn't care. She had both her parents—wasn't that enough? Why did she have all the luck—a Mommy and Daddy, sisters and brothers to play with, and we had nothing? Was it fair?

Of course not, Malky and I decided late one night, whispering in bed after the Kagan sisters' even breathing told us they were asleep. Though there were two other girls in our small town who were also motherless, they at least had one parent.

"But we also have a daddy," Malky whispered, clutching my hand. She had climbed into my bed for security and comfort. Usually, when she fell asleep I would toss and turn, uncomfortable because she was taking up too much room.

"Daddy? He doesn't care about us," I bitterly replied. "Leah, why don't you and Malky come and join our family?" I mimicked his offer. "He even forgot that my favorite name is Rina."

"He hasn't seen us in a long time," Malky whispered. "I miss him."

"How can you miss him? You were so little when he left! If you miss him, you can go live with him!" I said.

"I'm not going anywhere without you," Malky replied, and she really meant it.

"If Daddy really wanted to see us, he could come and visit," I continued, raising my voice.

"How could he come? He has his own family," Malky said, reasonably. "Besides, where would he stay?" The little house our family had rented, which contained our favorite furniture and all our memories, was now occupied by someone else. The table and chairs had been sold; everything else was too worn and chipped to be of any use.

"He could stay here, with us," I said unreasonably.

"Sure," said Malky, sarcastically. "Great idea."

"Sha!" Shira mumbled, in her sleep. Her two little sisters slept like logs, but she was a light sleeper.

Malky and I froze; she scooted to her bed, afraid that Shira would discover us shmoozing and want to know what we were talking about. We were not interested in telling her about our feelings, and made that extremely clear.

Time passed. Life with our aunt and uncle was bearable; it had even become routine. Though the numbness wore off and the pain diminished, the anger was always there. I was mad—at Daddy for not caring enough, at Aunt Shifra for taking us in, and strangely enough, at Mommy for dying and leaving us alone. I was even angry at myself, and I did not know why.

The teachers at school were understanding, and my friends were still there, as always. Not that I was such a loyal pal—I frequently preferred Malky's company to theirs. Still, they accepted me as I was. Anyway, once my mother died I felt different, although I couldn't really explain why. But I had trouble talking to my old friends. There were too many horrible things that had happened to me and all my friends had such normal quiet lives.

Things might have continued this way indefinitely, (I mean, until I grew up and got married,) if I hadn't rocked the boat. (Of course it was *bashert*, predestined, but my behavior definitely played a significant role in the matter).

Out of the blue, against my better judgment, as I grew older I began acting fresh and resistant to the adults around me. I would refuse to do my chores, or do them sullenly, and try to get away with a minimum of homework. As an almost twelve-year-old these *chutzpadig* incidences were not so funny, and nobody thought they were.

Uncle Michael jokingly called my attitude "teenage growing pains," but as time went by, he was less and less amused.

Hurtful, foolish comments would thoughtlessly slip from my mouth at the slightest provocation. The anger was raging inside me, threatening to explode. I hated the world. I hated the situation Malky and I had been forced into. In hindsight, I was too young and foolish to realize how it would have helped me to talk about my feelings with an understanding adult, someone who really cared, like my teacher Miss Hart. Though she was nearly in her sixties, she had never married, and wore her white hair in a bun. She was wise in the ways of the world, and always had something nice to say.

"You're carrying a very heavy load," she informed me, one afternoon, as I sat in detention for coming late for the third day in a row. "It's too much for one little girl."

I shrugged, not even bothering to reply.

"You want to show the world that you're big and strong, but you're doing it all wrong," she said, talking in rhymes. "It doesn't pay to keep it inside, from whom are you trying to hide?"

Miss Hart made lots of sense. I should have taken her words to heart, but I didn't.

Taking my lead, Malky became distant and rebellious as well. Our unspoken attitude: Who are these people, telling us what to do? Never mind that they were supporting us; we didn't need their help, or so we kidded ourselves. We could manage quite well on our own, we reasoned. Mommy had left us some money that was being held in an account supervised by Aunt Shifra and Uncle Michael, our legal guardians.

"We could take the money, run away, and live alone," I fantasized with Malky, plotting an elaborate plan for escape.

"It won't work," said my realistic sister. "We're too young. Let's wait another few years."

Though I was warned repeatedly—by teachers, by my principal, even by Uncle Michael—my attitude did not improve. They all used the same tactic; lecturing me about how I should appreciate all that my aunt and uncle were doing for us. Whoopy do! The poor little motherless girl is jumping for joy! If you think we're so lucky, why don't you try being practically an orphan, I felt like saying.

With our behavior, we sealed our own doom. It became too much of a burden for Uncle Michael and Aunt Shifra to bear. They were supporting their own large and growing family on a tight budget, and we were two extra, unappreciative mouths to feed. Then with the birth of the twins, it became clear that something would be done.

One thing led to another, until the fateful conversation that would change our lives forever, hurling us from the serene environment of our small town into a completely new life, leaving the familiar behind. Now we were to be placed in yet another home, like little plastic figures on the chess board. Oh, well.

When the preparations for our move began in earnest, Malky and I were taken shopping for new outfits.

"You don't really need a new outfit," Aunt Shifra said to me, pushing the twin carriage. "The Steins, where you'll be going, have lots of money and I'm sure they'll get you a new wardrobe."

"Then don't get me anything," I snapped. "Save it for Malky."

"But I don't want the Steins to think that I'm sending you like a beggar," she replied. "All I need for them to say is that I didn't take care of you."

We walked along the main street of our little town, each absorbed in her own thoughts.

"Who are the Steins, and how did you find them?" I asked.

"Oh, it's a long story," said Aunt Shifra, looking uncomfortable. "It goes back many years, when your mother and I came to America from Russia, when Uncle David was a little boy. Beth—that's Mrs. Stein—was like a mother to us. But things have changed since then. We're not on such good terms anymore. In fact, I was against the idea of your going there, but Uncle Michael and the Steins insisted."

"Why didn't you consult with me?" I demanded. But the instant the words came out of my mouth, I regretted them. Aunt Shifra paled. "Sorry, forget it," I said. Just then one twin began to cry, and I popped the pacifier into her mouth. The topic was not brought up again.

Yet the questions remained. So many questions...

"Attention all passengers, please fasten your seat belts. All passengers, fasten your seat belts. The plane will be landing at J.F.K. in fifteen minutes."

I awoke from my reverie, in a daze. Had I really been dreaming that long? Though I had been sitting motionless for the past hour, I felt exhausted, as if I had spent that time lifting heavy weights. And perhaps I had.

The plane slowly descended and then circled over the airport. I looked out the window at the long coastline and then the skyscrapers of the big city. It was all so big and forbidding. How would I fit in? The wheels of the plane touched the ground, jolting me, infusing me with a surge of excitement. I had arrived!

Starting Over

Soon the passengers were lining up in the center of the plane and bustling about reaching into the overhead compartments for their carry-on bags. As soon as the airplane door was opened, we poured down the ramp.

"New York City—here I come!" I walked quickly down the ramp.

"Can't you watch where you're going? Don't bump into other people!" an annoyed voice at my elbow said as she moved away from me and disappeared quickly into the crowd.

"Does she think I'm a pickpocket?" I wondered aloud. A smiling stewardess, who had surveyed the scene, quickly set me straight.

"Welcome to New York! Manners don't count much over here. From now on, it's everyone for themselves. Lots of people don't even bother saying 'sorry' or helping an old lady cross the street. Here you watch out just for yourself!" I raised my eyebrows at her. I felt so grown up arriving by myself in a big city and getting advice about how to survive! Wait until I told Malky!

I walked through the teeming concourse, trying to be unfazed by the commotion, even though I was dumfounded. The woman with the crying baby who had sat behind me hurried ahead, and was greeted by a fan club consisting of what looked to be grandpa and grandma.

"Look who's here! If it isn't Laura and the darling baby! Welcome!"

I looked away, quickly, ignoring the sinking feeling in the pit of my stomach. In my hand I clutched a small piece of paper that read "Gate 6". Uncle Michael had warned me to stay at that gate, since the travel agent said it was not too far from where my plane was arriving. My new guardians, the Steins would come and fetch me by this gate.

"I understand they have a chauffeur who drives them," Uncle Michael had said, in all seriousness. "But I'm sure they'll want to come and pick you up in person. They were supposed to come and pick you up from our home, but since they just arrived from a business trip in Europe a short while ago, it didn't work out."

Apparently, the Steins had two homes—one somewhere in Europe and one in New York. They ran a thriving business, something to do with financial investing, and traveled a lot. They also had one married son, living in Europe. They were very eager to give me a home, but did not have much experience with girls my age. I had gleaned these details from careful inquiries and listening to conversations during the week before my departure. But there was so much I didn't know. Aunt Shifra's short explanation during our shopping trip was only the tip of the iceberg.

There were so many questions I still had...But now I needed to get my luggage, which was being held near Gate 11.

Everyone seemed to be in a hurry. People were snatching their bags from the conveyer belt like vultures, or paying porters to help them with their bags. There weren't many families waiting at "arrivals" to greet the passengers. This was mainly a business flight, and I was among the few young people on board.

When my suitcase with all my precious belongings finally arrived, I lugged it myself—no need to hire the porters who walked faster than you could follow—and followed the throng, puffing and panting all the way to Gate 6.

I waited...and waited...and waited some more. I

hopped from one foot to another, hummed a little tune, and surveyed the crowd impatiently. Could it be that couple over there? Nah, Mrs. Stein wouldn't be wearing a tattered jacket, and I'm sure her husband doesn't wear Nike sneakers. I stifled a giggle as the couple stared at me for an instant, and then walked off. Who was I looking for, exactly? I wasn't sure myself.

Six o'clock on an autumn evening. The crowd began to thin. Most of the travelers had gone outside to hail a cab, and the few remaining ones did not look like they had anywhere to go. I began to get nervous, I mean, really nervous. Where were they?

I've got to find a pay phone, I decided, and call either the folks back home or the Steins. Just as I was about to do so, another thought popped into my head.

"How about surprising the Steins and arriving by yourself?"

"Don't be silly," I brushed the thought away. "They'll be worried stiff about you."

"But you're already waiting over an hour," the voice protested. "Besides, are you sure you have the right gate?"

"Sure I'm sure. And Uncle Michael warned me to stay at the gate until they come."

"Do you plan to stay here all night? Don't be naive!"

I waited another ten minutes, and by then was

so impatient, so fueled with resolve, that I pulled my suitcase after me, and walked outside into the gathering dusk.

The New York airport was a busy place, I soon discovered.

My ears tingled with the vibrations of traffic, laughter and business talk surrounding me on all sides. Still, I stood alone, trying to figure out where the cabs were. Finally I walked over to a big sign that said "taxi stand."

"Anabody needa cab?" a cabbie shouted, leaning his head out the window of a big yellow cab. His teeth looked almost black and he was chewing an enormous cigar. A tall woman in a business suit who stood ahead of me shook her head. Disappointed, he began to drive away. I snapped out of my reverie....

"Wait! I need a taxi!" I must have yelled out loud, because several people turned. The cabbie eyed me suspiciously. "Y'know where y'goin?"

"Yes." Uncle Michael had written the Steins' address and phone number clearly on a piece of paper. I handed him the slip. "You know the way, don't you?"

"Sure. Like the back of my hand. It's about half an hour's ride from here. It'll be twenty dollars for the trip. You got the money?"

I still had forty dollars left over after my taxi ride from the train station to the airplane. I pulled the money out of my wallet and showed it to him.

Mr. Cabbie helped me stow my suitcase in the trunk, and I sank into the back seat, suddenly weary.

As the car sped along, I gazed unseeingly at the monotonous gray of the highway, pondering my situation. What a day! First I had taken a train, then a taxi, then a plane and now another taxi all by myself. I was certainly growing up fast!

As the skies began to darken, so did my mood. My former ebullience and "grown up" attitude quickly faded away, as it became clear that I had gotten myself into a lot of hot water. For one thing, I couldn't imagine that this woman, whom Uncle Michael called my "aunt", really wanted me. She undoubtedly was only taking me out of a sense of duty to my mother. She probably felt sorry for me. After all, why would she want to go through all this trouble at her age! I had spoken to her once, a week before, and sensed that she made a supreme effort to be friendly.

Involuntarily shuddering, I busied myself by straightening my crumpled skirt and retying my shoelaces. I surreptitiously licked my fingers and wiped them on my sneakers in a heroic effort to clean what looked like layers of mud. My shirt was tucked in, my curly red hair smoothed. I then closed my eyes and nodded off to sleep.

By the time I opened my eyes twenty minutes

later, the sky was darkening. The road had narrowed, leaving room for bushes and grass on either side. The trees were shedding their foliage, but there were no leaves piled in clumps on the ground.

We had entered a well-to-do area, with large, beautiful homes gracing each side of the street. There were lots of big lawns and room in between the houses. The streets were well lit by pretty brass lamps, but were devoid of people. Only an occasional car joined us, eventually disappearing into smaller blocks.

The taxi paused only for a second, then pulled into a side street. The street sign read Elm Drive. My heart beat faster; this must be it! The Steins lived at number 18.

The narrow street looked like all the rest, only a bit plainer, with nondescript brick houses clustered closer together and smaller lawns in the front. The streetlights cast a yellowish glow on the homes, and illuminated the numbers on the front doors.

The cab driver pulled over at number 18, and I craned my neck to catch a glimpse. We were in the driveway of a reddish stucco house with overgrown bushes surrounding the small front lawn. It didn't look so rich or fancy but I thought maybe for New York it was.

"So, whaddya know? I know New York like the back of my hand. What did ah tell you? Is this the right house?"

"Well, um...I think so," I replied, handing him a twenty dollar bill.

"Don't ya live here?" The cab driver turned around and was staring at me with curiosity.

I didn't bother answering. Silently, the cabbie removed my suitcase from the trunk. I got out of the car and then he drove off. I was alone.

There was no car in the driveway, and the house was nothing special. Strange. Were they (gasp) at the airport looking for me? If so, I was in big trouble.

I left my suitcase near the curb and squared my shoulders, walking with measured steps up the graveled front path. There were three stairs to climb before I faced the front door of heavy varnished wood. There was no sign on the door, save a large *mezuzah* and the number 18. I paused for a moment, then lifted the heavy brass knocker.

I heard the slow, steady sound of steps coming toward the door, and the door was opened. Facing me was an old lady with the whitest hair I had ever seen, and there were cat's eye spectacles perched on her nose. She squinted twice before focusing on me, giving me a warm smile.

I stared back in surprise and shock. Uncle Michael had assured me that my aunt wasn't young, but not old enough to be my grandmother. I didn't imagine her to be so ancient...and so friendly.

"This couldn't be the right house," a voice inside me warned. "There must have been some mistake."

I stuck my hand in my pocket, reaching for the paper with the address on it. I grew frantic when I realized that I had given it to the cabbie.

What choice did I have now? It was already late and the taxi had left. The smartest thing to do was to go into the house and call Uncle Michael for the address.

The little old woman stared me up and down for a few minutes.

"Oh, it's you, darling? What a nice surprise! Goodness, *mein kindt*, why don't you come in, darling? I'll fix you some tea!" she said ushering me in with bustling warmth. I smiled at her, and she smiled back. Suddenly, I realized that this sweet old lady had probably mistaken me for someone else.

"Uh....I think that we have a little mix-up here...," I stammered.

Her back was to me, and apparently she didn't hear.

I followed her inside, entering an untidy living room, scattered with crocheted sweaters and knitting needles. Altogether, there was a homey look about the place.

"Darling, I'm so glad to see you!" she said in an accented English, bobbing her white head up and down. "Why don't you come into the kitchen with me while I fix your tea?" She guided me into a small room with a sink and cabinets, and sat me down at the kitchen table while she set the kettle on the stove. I decided to play along with the game, and enjoy it while it lasted. I was sure this was not my aunt.

While the water was warming, she kept up a steady chatter, never pausing for a reply. She talked about how lonely she had been, who she had seen in shul this past Shabbos and how happy she was that I had finally arrived. All this time, I was so curious I could burst. Who was this woman?

Finally, the kettle was steaming, and the old lady slowly poured the boiled water into a drinking glass, sprinkling it liberally with sugar. She dunked a tea bag in seven times, and when it was a deep, dark color, she brought it to the table and set it before me.

Could I drink this? Was it kosher? I knew from the *mezuzah* on the door and from her speech that she surely was Jewish—but how could I be sure that she kept kosher?

"Excuse me..." I stammered. "I think that we have a mis—"

But she didn't even seem to have heard me, she was so busy staring at me.

Suddenly, her happy expression changed to one of bewilderment. "Oh, my, Kreindel. Why is your hair so short? You used to have such pretty curls! What entered your *kepele* to cut it off? Tell your grandma why you would do such a thing!"

My heart skipped a beat.

"My name isn't Kreindel, ma'am," I replied, trying to suppress a smile. "And I've always had short hair. And," I emphasized, "You aren't my grandma."

"*Vus iz dus!*" the old woman replied, startled. She adjusted her glasses on her nose and stared harder, slow realization dawning on her face. "So...you...you aren't my Kreindel after all!"

"No, I'm afraid not."

"Oy, vey! Darling, we've made some mistake!"

"Yes, I'm afraid we have."

The little old lady screwed up her face. I was afraid she would begin to cry. "There, there now," I interrupted, beginning to understand. "Is Kreindel your granddaughter?"

"Yes...my only grandchild. Oh my, oh my...Now you will go away and leave me all alone!"

My heart went out to this woman, and I wished I could be her granddaughter. "Please don't be so upset. Maybe I can help you," I begged. She looked so forlorn and alone—just like me.

Her shoulders stopped shaking, and little by little, she calmed down. She removed an embroidered handkerchief from her pocket and blew into it vigorously. At length, she looked up and I noticed her red-rimmed eyes.

"What did you say, darling? I didn't hear you."

"I said that you shouldn't be so sad. Maybe Kreindel will still come."

"But whose little girl are you?"

"I am nobody's little girl," I replied with a gulp and then realized how melodramatic it sounded. But it was true so I continued. "My mother died, my father lives far away and my sister lives in London, so now I'm all alone."

"Your Mommy is not living? How sad!" Then with determination the old woman said, "Then you must come live with me, darling."

She stretched her arms wide, and continued, "My house is your house. It is nice and comfortable, and you can have your own room—the one in which my Kreindel stays," she ended on a hopeful note.

I must say that I was sorely tempted to take the offer. I could see right now that life with this grandma would probably be all honey and roses. Cinnamon buns for breakfast, and the companionship of an sweet old woman! I mentally surveyed the untidy kitchen. Of course, the first thing that had to be done was to wash those dishes. And then the wallpaper was peeling. I must see to the floor....

"I see you like my house already!" the woman exclaimed with pride, her spectacles slipping down her nose. I instinctively reached out to adjust them and she patted my hand lovingly.

"Where do you come from darling?"

I was momentarily taken aback. The question hit me full force, reminding me that I had arrived at the wrong address. I had been spinning a rosy web around this old woman, and I didn't even know her name. Besides, the Steins must be frantic by now.

"Uh...what is your name?" I asked shyly.

"I am Mrs. Kassel," she said, stressing the last syllable. "I live here already for thirty-five years, and my kitchen is strictly kosher. As Harold, my dear husband, of blessed memory, used to say, 'even a Rabbi can eat in our home.' You look like a nice, *frum* girl, and I could use some company. Maybe you want to stay with me?"

"Uh...I guess I have to make a phone call," I could only stammer in reply.

"Here's the phone. Ask your family if you can stay with me, Gertrude Kassel, on 18 Elm Drive. Oh, I am so excited! I'm going upstairs right now to change the linen on the bed in the spare room!"

She left me in the kitchen and started up the stairs, pausing by every other stair to catch her breath. I guess it never even dawned on her that my aunt and uncle might object.

I carefully dialed the Kagan's number on her phone, putting my fingers into the holes of the old rotary dial. I waited an agonizing few minutes, and then heard the unmistakable buzz of a busy signal.

I could hear Mrs. Kassel puttering upstairs. I waited a few minutes and dialed again. The phone barely rang before my worried-sounding aunt picked up.

"Hello? Aunt Shifra! Is that you?"

"Leah? Hi! I'm so relieved to hear your voice! The

Steins were looking for you! How was your trip? Are you all settled already?"

I could barely get a word in edgewise.

"Aunt Shifra?"

"Yes?"

"I'm....I don't know how to say this, but I'm not at Aun—"

"You're what? Where are you? Did you get lost?" Aunt Shifra began to sound frantic.

"No, I'm not lost, or not in the way you imagine. I just ended up at the wrong house—"

"Where are you?" her voice rose an octave.

"18 Elm Drive!" I shouted into the phone.

"How did you get there? The Steins live at 18 Elm Place!" she replied. "Didn't they pick you up at the airport?"

"No, they didn't. I waited almost two hours, and then decided to take a taxi," I said, utterly spent. "By mistake, the cabbie took me to the wrong address, and I knocked at an old lady's door. She's the sweetest old lady you ever saw, and I think she's half blind and half deaf. Anyway she mistook me for her grandchild. She has been so nice to me! She even offered that I could stay with her."

"Oh, I knew I should never have let you travel alone. Leah, repeat everything again, and clearly this time. I want to know exactly what happened since you got off the airplane."

"Well, I took a taxi and told him the address, and

he took me to 18 Elm Drive, only it wasn't where Aunt Beth lives at all. A little old lady answered the door and thought I was her grandchild, and...."

"And the rest you told me already. Now take a pen and paper and write down the phone number I tell you. And don't lose it! Call the Steins immediately and tell them where you are! Call me as soon as you get there!"

Aunt Shifra sounded too annoyed—and furious—to listen to anything else I had to say. I picked up the phone again, and dialed the number she gave me.

The phone rang and rang and then a machine picked up with a polite, efficient-sounding message..

"Hello, you have reached the Stein residence. We are sorry we are unavailable to take your call. Please leave a message after the tone."

I felt ready to cry. Stifling my tears, I managed to croak into the phone.

"Hi, it's me, Rina Leah Berger. There was a mistake—sorry. I'm stuck at 18 Elm—"

My rambling was interrupted by a crisp woman's voice who picked up the phone, mid-message.

"Hello, is that Leah?"

"Yes, it's me," I said, relieved.

"Where are you? Mr. and Mrs. Stein have been waiting at the airport for hours!"

"I'm at 18 Elm Drive, and I got here by mistake.

I'm so sorry! It's, oh, it's a long story," I said.

"As long as you're safe, *boruch Hashem*," said the female voice. I wondered who she was. "Elm Drive isn't too far from Elm Place, where we live. As soon as Butch gets back from the airport—wait, I think I hear them in the driveway. Yes, they're back. I'll tell Butch to come and get you right away."

She put down the phone and I placed the receiver gingerly in its cradle, suddenly feeling extremely nervous.

Mrs. Kassel's muffled voice suddenly called out, "Dearie, would you come up and help me do the linens?"

I raced up the stairs two at a time, distinctly aware of the musty odor. The bedrooms were dark and airless. There was a single light shining down the carpeted hallway, and I followed.

"Dearie, are you coming?" Mrs. Kassel called.

"Coming!" I yelled, racing towards the room, then pausing at the doorway. The room was painted in various shades of pink, with a design of ivy leaves on the walls. The wooden furniture was worn out and tired looking. Nothing about the room seemed particularly inviting, yet I loved it because I knew that I was needed here.

I glanced around for a second, before realizing that Mrs. Kassel was standing behind the fluffy lump of bed linen piled in the corner. Her scratchy voice came from behind it, "Oh, my, dearie. I'm having a hard time with the comforters... Will you help me?"

I could barely make out her voice, stifled as it was behind the heavy comforter. I swallowed a giggle.

"Sure I'll help you with the cover," and I struggled to fix it. Finally, the bed was smoothed down.

"Oh, dearie, next time I'll let you to do this job," she panted, out of breath. Her cheeks were red with exertion.

"I don't know about a next time—" I began, when we were interrupted by the sound of a honking horn.

I raced to the grimy window, and squinted out. There was a black Lincoln Town Car honking in her driveway.

The older woman followed me to the window, peering over my shoulder. "Oh my, oh my, oh, ooh! What is making all that noise? I think you should go to check."

I felt awful! How in the world was I to disappoint this new-found friend? If only there was some way....

Honk! Honk! The Lincoln Town Car driver was getting impatient. I made out the outline of a man getting out of the driver's seat and walking up to the door....

I raced down the stairs, slid open the great upper lock and turned the doorknob.

A tall and stiff-looking man stood at the door. He

was clean shaven with a pair of expressionless brown eyes. So this was the chauffeur. My gosh! What must it feel like to have a driver take you wherever you want to go?

We stood there, scrutinizing each other silently. His face was impassive, which gave him a haughty air.

"Are you the person that's supposed to pick me up?" I wanted to ask, but something held me back. Instead I kept quiet.

"I'm here to pick up a girl by the name of 'Leah Berger.'"

"Leah Berger?"

I could hear the slippered footsteps of the older woman thumping down the stairs. She walked straight up to the man, her head barely reaching his shoulders. Squinting unevenly, she peered into his eyes.

"Ah, if it isn't my Haskel! Come in you naughty boy! Where have you been until now?"

The man looked confused for a minute and then a look of understanding softened his face.

"Alzheimer's," he muttered, stifling a smile.

"Alz where? Haskele, I've been waiting for you, *mein kindt*. Come and see the delicious cinnamon buns I baked for you." The man stepped back.

Mrs. Kassel stretched out her arms, looking him straight in the eye. Suddenly, she shrank back.

"Oy, did you cut off your beard, Haskel? A nice

Jewish boy like you?!?" The man reddened with embarrassment."

"Mrs. Kassel," I said, my voice quavering. "I don't think this is your Haskel."

She looked up a little stunned at first and then she looked contrite.

"Oh, I'm sorry, young man. I think I made a mistake. Only, you look so much like my Haskel, even without the beard. Shall I show you a picture of my Haskel?"

"That won't be necessary," he said, annoyed, obviously waiting for me to get moving. But Mrs. Kassel had already gone to the dining room and I followed.

The man's patience soon ran out. With a sense of purpose and the same lack of expression, he strode into the dining room and stood before us, waiting.

"Now look here. Are you Miss Leah?..."

"Well, I guess so."

"Then will you please come with me?

Resolutely, I turned to go, bid Mrs. Kassel goodbye and promised to visit her again. I even gave her a tiny kiss and actually felt forlorn leaving her.

"I'll miss you too, darling! Come visit me!" were her parting words.

Luckily, my battered suitcase was still in front of the house. The man, who introduced himself as Butch took it, (did I sense his distaste?) and securely stowed it in the trunk. I wasn't sure where to sit but Butch opened the back door for me so I climbed into the back seat. We rode in silence. The butter-flies dancing in my stomach were making me feel sick. I didn't want to think of what was to come.

Butch pulled up near a long finely graveled dri-veway, lit by two gas lamps throwing an oily glow on the lawn.

"Is this the house, Butch?"

"Yep, Miss Leah."

Miss Leah. I couldn't get used to the name. And I couldn't get used to the house. It must have been the biggest house I had ever seen. It looked like a mansion. When they said my aunt and uncle were rich they weren't kidding!

The house was set back from the street, and built of severe gray brick and granite. Two massive portals towered above me. Everything about the house appeared cold.

A thin ray of light shone from one window; oth-erwise, the house was shrouded in darkness. Mommy had usually left some lights on at night, making me feel secure. My heart skipped a giant beat as Butch opened the door with a key, holding my heavy suitcase as if it were a balloon.

"Coming, Miss?" he called after me. I reluctantly dragged my feet up the front stairs, and stood on the porch near the doorway. I had arrived at my new home.

Inside
The Mansion

he door swung open, and I kissed the *mezuzah*, walking into the largest foyer I had ever seen. And when I say large, I mean really huge—bigger than our dining room back home. Bigger than any dining room I'd ever seen. (Which isn't really saying much at all.) A sparkling crystal chandelier hung from the ceiling, and a marble-topped table in the corner held a large and stunning bouquet of fresh flowers. Another silk arrangement was cleverly arranged in an alcove in the wall.

I noticed these details out of the corner of my eye, as I stood, tongue tied, staring at the couple who had decided to give me a home—for directly in front of me were my uncle and aunt.

"Welcome, Leah!" said the elegant woman who I knew must be my aunt. She came forward, engulfing me in her embrace. I gingerly hugged her back. "You can call me Aunt Beth, and this," she pointed to her husband, "is Uncle Gerald."

"Now, now, Beth," her husband intervened. "Don't smother her!" We all laughed nervously, glad that he had lightened the air.

"Your Aunt Shifra has told me what a wonderful girl you are," Mrs. Stein continued, keeping a hand on my shoulder. "When we spoke on the phone, I tried to imagine what you look like. I must say, you're even prettier than I imagined," she said.

"Thank you," I stammered, at a loss for a reply. Then she took a step back, and we looked at each other for a long moment. Mrs. Stein, (or Aunt Beth?) wore a silk patterned blouse and a pleated navy skirt. Her blue pumps were the exact shade of her skirt, and a diamond choker and diamond stud earrings complemented her outfit. But the face...it was that of a middle-aged woman, with some slight wrinkles on her forehead and a hard set to her chin. Her eyes were gray and unflinching, and she seemed to be sharp and alert as she examined me. I had a feeling that here was a woman who was extremely intelligent and used to having everything done her way.

"Welcome to our home, Leah," Mr. Stein came forward, beaming effusively. "We've been trying to track you down all evening. I say, 'all's well that ends well.'"

"I'm sorry," I stammered, and really meant it. It was hard to mistake the friendliness and genuine warmth that shone out of his eyes.

Slighter and thinner than his wife, Mr. Stein had graying sideburns, a brown, scraggly beard and an affectionate, open face. I liked the warmth of his deep brown eyes immediately. Though he wore designer glasses and an elegant silk tie, his suit was ever so slightly rumpled looking. He stifled a yawn.

"Excuse me, it's been a long day," he said, after an awkward pause. "Let's go to the living room for a snack and you can tell us all about the mix-up."

I followed them gingerly, my silent footsteps in contrast to the clickety click of Aunt Beth's heels. We passed an enormous dining room, whose rich hardwood floor had centered on it a large intricately-designed Oriental carpet. The furniture looked antique and expensive, almost like a furniture showroom or something.

The sunken living room was adjacent to the dining room, its dim lighting accenting the thick wall-to-wall carpeting and plush white silk couches. Mrs. Stein flicked on the light switch, and the room suddenly took shape and form before my eyes. The furniture was so formal, neatly arranged in a precise pattern. The curio cabinet took up one wall, and was filled with lots of sparkling silver pieces.

The Steins sat down on the white couch and were waiting for me to sit.

"It's...so...elegant," I stammered, fumbling for the right words.

"Well thank you, Leah. We had a wonderful decorator helping us," Mrs. Stein said, smiling with her mouth only. (I knew I shouldn't be so judgmental. But there was something fake about her smile.)

"So tell us about your day," Uncle Gerald (I guess that's what I'll call him) queried, breaking the awkward pause.

"Nothing much. Uh...I woke up at six, got my stuff, I mean, finished packing my suitcase, took a cab to the train station, traveled a few hours, took another cab to the airport..." I recited these events matter of factly, as though they had happened to someone else. The Steins listened carefully, not interrupting my monologue.

"Is this the first time your uncle and aunt let you travel all by yourself?" My aunt wrinkled her nose in distaste.

My cheeks flushed, as I felt myself being attacked.

"Of course," I said proudly. "But I'm not a kid anymore. I'm almost thirteen."

"Thirteen is a still a child in my books," Aunt Beth replied. "We wanted to come pick you up, but your aunt wouldn't hear of it."

"Beth—I don't think—," her husband cut in.

Hmm...that's interesting. Aunt Shifra claimed they couldn't come because they had just come back from Europe. I wondered whose version was correct.

"In any case, what's done is done," Mrs. Stein continued. "We spent all evening trying to track you down, waiting at the airport and wondering where you were."

"Don't make her feel guilty," Uncle Gerald admonished. "*Boruch Hashem* she's here with us, and that's what matters."

I shot him a grateful look. I had a funny feeling that he would be coming to my rescue in the future as well. Just a foreboding that might prove to be unfounded. Then again, I've learned the hard way that life is unpredictable.

"Let me tell you a little bit about our home," Uncle Gerald continued, in a softer tone. "Now that our son, Boruch, is married and living in Belgium, it's just the two of us, Beth and me. We run a financial consulting business, and travel to Europe quite a bit. Since we're there so often, we have our own home there as well. In fact, we returned from there only a week ago, but we won't need to go back for a while."

He paused for breath, and continued. "Our business is very complicated, with many employees, and keeps us busy for most of the week. Beth doesn't usually get home until seven in the evening, and

I sometimes make it home by eight."

"Which gives us a suppertime of eight fifteen," Aunt Beth cut in crisply. "Of course, we have hired help, and you won't be expected to do a thing. Judith is our housekeeper, and we call her Jenny. A fine Jewish girl, she's been with us for a number of years. She's extremely reliable and thoughtful. Recently she's been complaining that the house-work and cooking are too much for her. We decided to hire a cook a couple of months ago who also does the shopping. Svetlana is a lovely, frum Russian woman, and since she's a widow, she moved in with us. She has become quite Americanized and insists we call her Susan. We have lots of guests on Shabbos and Susan cooks up a feast. She's totally taken over the kitchen, and sometimes helps Jenny with the housekeeping as well. Neither of them does the heavy scrubbing. A cleaning lady comes in once a week for that."

"Wow," was all I could muster. I guess coming from the small Midwestern town where I grew up with my mother and sister in a plain little two-bed-room house, this was a bit too much for me. Maids to do all the wok? Two homes on different conti-nents? Living in a mansion?

"Don't let it overwhelm you," Uncle Gerald added thoughtfully. "We understand that you aren't used to such a big house," he said, reading my mind. "But as you'll see, the people who work in our

house are more like family. Even Butch. He's our
chauffeur and doubles as a handyman. With a
house as large as ours there are always some odds
and ends that only a man like him can attend to."

With a house like ours. Even from where I sat, I
could see the hallway branch off into two direc-
tions, leading to doorways and staircases...it made
me dizzy. But suddenly, I felt my stomach rum-
bling. I was starved.

"Leah, are you hungry?" Aunt Beth asked solicitously. "You probably have not had a thing to eat
today. You must be famished. Come into the
kitchen and I'll have Susan prepare you a meal."

She stood up, walked over to the intercom, and
flicked on the switch.

"Susan...please come into the kitchen," she said
in an authoritative voice.

Almost instantly, the sound of pattering footsteps was heard upstairs, as I followed Aunt Beth
into the kitchen. The room was huge and the decor
looked so modern, even futuristic. The marble-tiled
floors were glossy and the highly polished oak cabinets shone under the powerful kitchen spotlights.

Uncle Gerald followed us, and as we waited for
Susan to arrive he walked over to the phone and
began a long, boring business call.

Aunt Beth pulled a notepad out of a sliding drawer and began to write a list. I just stood there.

As soon as Susan walked into the room I felt the

warmth that emanated from her smile. She looked to be about sixty, full figured with frizzy gray hair covered with a colorful kerchief. Her house dress was decorated with the same design, complementing her deep blue eyes. When she grinned at me her entire face seemed to light up, shooting sparks of sunshine to the room.

"Ah, welcome to the new member in our family," she said in a heavily Russian accent, spreading her arms wide. "We're so happy to see you."

She hugged me and patted my back, making me feel like a long lost relative who had finally arrived, which, I guess, in fact, I was.

"So, you've just arrived, huh?" she said, bustling about the kitchen, donning her apron and going over to the extra large stove where two pots were simmering. She opened the enormous two-door silver fridge and took out a salad and a beautiful decorated plate of liver.

"Leave it to Susan," Aunt Beth said, smiling briefly, then turning back to her list. I was grateful for her preoccupation, which meant that perhaps I could eat without having her stare at me, which made me feel so uncomfortable.

"Sit down and eat," Susan urged, setting a plate of fresh liver and rice in front of me. I got up and washed, made a *bracha* and took a bite of the bread. Then I tasted the liver and rice. Mmmm...the food tasted as good as it looked. Within no time, it was gone.

I was so absorbed in my meal that at first I didn't realize Aunt Beth was scrutinizing my every move. When I finally looked up and met her gaze we both looked away.

With the next course, a mushroom and chicken soufflé and some baby corn and peas, I was a bit more careful, wiping my fingers on a napkin and taking delicate bites. Of course, since I wasn't so hungry anymore, it was easier to be polite. I didn't want my aunt to think I was some country bumpkin. Dessert was amazing and I had to struggle not to eat quickly. A fruit salad with raspberry ices. Everything tasted incredible.

"All done?" Susan asked kindly, pouring me a tall glass of ginger ale. She seemed to enjoy watching me eat, *shepping nachas* from the way I savored her food.

"Yes, thank you, it was delicious," I said, in between sips of the once-forbidden soda. The food had made me tired, and I covered a yawn with my hand.

Aunt Beth looked at the clock. "It's so late already!" she exclaimed. "Come, I'll show you to your room."

I *bentched* and began to clear my plate.

"Please, don't worry about it!" said Susan. "Clearing away is my job. You go up and rest."

Wow! And wow again! Imagine not having to clear

your plate!

Of course, although I didn't say anything out loud, my expression must have given me away.

"You're an honored member of our family, Leah," said Aunt Beth, smiling and placing an arm on my shoulder. "Just do your best to make us proud and leave the meals and cleaning up to Susan."

I flinched, wondering at the implied responsibility in her words. How in the world was I supposed to make them proud?

"Come, let me take you to your room," she repeated. Uncle Gerald had put down the phone and bid me good night. "Enjoy the first night in your new room," he said, smiling. "Your aunt furnished it especially for you."

I smiled, then turned toward the hallway, eyes searching for my suitcase. Hadn't Butch left it in the hallway?

"What are you looking for?" Aunt Beth asked.

"Oh...uh...I...just my suitcase," I said.

"Jenny must have taken it up to your room," she replied, raising her voice. "Jenny?"

"Coming!" Her voice came from nearby. I turned, and stared at the woman that entered. Her coal black eyes accentuated a long, thin face, and she seemed to be about thirty. Her black hair was pulled back with a hairpin, and she was dressed in a simple blue house dress, yet it was immaculately clean. She wore an unmistakable "no nonsense" air, and I found it difficult to smile at her. Yet I did. She instantly smiled back.

"Welcome to our home, Leah. I'm so glad you're here!"

End of welcome. Jenny didn't look like she had anything to say to me. She turned to my aunt.

"Beth, there seems to be a problem with the table arrangements at the conference," she said, speaking in a crisp, official manner. "Lucy just called from the office with a revised guest list."

I stood tapping my feet impatiently, as my aunt and uncle became absorbed in the discussion about some business conference. Susan finally took pity on me.

"I'll show Leah to her room, poor thing, she must be exhausted."

"Oh, of course, I'm sorry," said a distracted Aunt Beth. "It's just that there's so much going on, and the conference will be next week—"

I nodded, making believe I understood. One thing was certain—my aunt and uncle definitely were preoccupied with their business. I seemed to have arrived at a busy time in their schedule, I thought as I followed Susan down the hall.

"Good night, Leah," Uncle Gerald called after me.

"Good night," I replied, hoping they were not angry at me for having forgotten to say it first.

Oh, well, can't think of everything. "Don't worry so much," an inner voice hissed.

"I can't help it," I hissed back.

"What were you saying?" Susan asked, already halfway up the majestic flight of carpeted stairs.

"N...nothing," I replied, clambering up after her. I gingerly touched the polished wooden banister, looking up at the crystal light fixture that hung from the second floor, a majestic ball right in the center of the landing.

At the top of the stairs, there was another foyer, which branched off into a few separate hallways.

"The Stein's suite is over in that direction," Susan said, gesturing toward the right. "And that—" she pointed down the hallway to the left, "will be your room."

"Where do you and Jenny sleep?" I asked.

"Oh, we're up in the third floor," she laughed. "Good exercise for me!'"

"Butch doesn't sleep here; he has his own family and only works here by day," Susan continued, as I followed her down the hallway.

"This is your room," Susan said sweeping her hand over the doorknob.

I stopped at the doorway, and closed my eyes for a minute to imagine what the room would look like. This was my favorite game, imagining exciting things just before they happened, then opening the surprise quickly and seeing if it matched my expectations.

For many years now, Malky and I had envisioned

a dream bedroom, and decorated and painted it to match our wildest fancy. So now I paused, with a thrill, and saw the room in my mind's eye....

The furniture would be decorated in mauve and pale yellow, from the frilly bedspreads and matching curtains to the doily on the writing desk in the corner. The walls would be painted with delicate yellow flowers to match. There'd be a tall, white bureau chest in one corner and a matching bookcase filled with games on the side....

My reverie had taken only an instant, time enough for Susan to open the door and flick on the light switch, stepping aside to let me pass. I stepped in, and blinked. Reality hit hard.

"B...but...it isn't a girl's bedroom at all! Why, it isn't even decorated!" I burst out in dismay.

Susan watched my expression of disappointment as I surveyed the silk maroon curtains, polished oaken armoire and four poster bed. A matching desk and chair took up one corner, and a bookcase (still empty) stood against the other wall.

"Why, Leah, this furniture is antique! Look at the antique gold knobs on the drawer pulls!"

I walked over to the dresser and gingerly patted one. It definitely looked handsome and dignified, but not the kind of room an almost thirteen-year-old like me would find herself at home in. Definitely not!

"It looks just like...a room for a king!" I declared,

and Susan nodded, proud of the description. "But I'm not a king! I'm only a plain girl!"

"Oh, but you're a member of the 'royal family'. I wish I had such a room," she said trying to mollify me.

"I'd love to change with you, Susan. I'm positive your room is so warm...and homelike. This is so cold...and distant."

"Cold? I'll put the steam up in an instant."

"No. Please don't!" I almost shouted. "I can't stand the steam!"

"Well, if you don't want me to, I won't." Susan looked hurt.

"I'm sorry, Susan. I didn't mean to offend you. It's just that....I'm a bit homesick and lonely...and tired..."

Susan looked at her watch. "It's way past your bedtime!" she gasped, horrified. "Quickly wash up in the shower and get into your nightclothes. You'll find all you need in the room. The nighties are under your pillow."

"My nightclothes? I think they're in my suitcase. I didn't unpack them yet."

"No need to. Mrs. Stein bought you an entire new wardrobe."

As she spoke, she walked over to the canopied bed, dug under the king size pillow, and removed a starched, crisp beige nightgown.

It looked anything but comfortable. And totally

not my style.

"I don't want to wear that, Susan. I'd rather wear my own things," I complained.

"Look here, now. I can't get your things up anymore. It's late and the Steins will want to know what the problem is. The last thing you need is having her come up to your room now," Susan spoke reasonably, as if trying to calm a cranky kid. "Wear it just for tonight, okay?"

"Okay. G'nite Susan."

"Goodnight dear. Sleep well."

I heard her footsteps recede down the hallway, and then I was alone. Alone in a giant, unfriendly room with my thoughts.

I washed up in the ivory bathroom with matching accessories, marveling at the luxury—my very own bathroom! I couldn't believe I didn't have to share the bathroom with anyone! Living with Aunt Shifra had meant long waits for the single bathroom. Wait until Malky heard! I brushed my hair and pulled on the scratchy nightgown. Then I gingerly climbed into the four poster bed and left the light on the night table on.

"*Shema Yisroel, Hashem Elokeinu Hashem Echod.*" How many times had Mommy *a"h* said *Krias Shema* with me, tucking me into bed? Malky and I would curl into our covers, as Mommy sang *Hamalach Hagoel* with a lilting melody.

Uch! Why do the tears have to come every time I

think of Mommy? Tears, tears, go away. Come back another day. Can't you see I'm tired? Let me sleep.

I gave a giant yawn, and was out like a light. And so the first night in my new home passed.

A New Start

Tuesday morning. The sun was streaming through the folds in the thick curtains, shining into my eyes. I opened my eyes wondering where I was. For an instant I couldn't remember how I had gotten to this strange room. Then it all came back. I was in my new bed, wearing my new nightgown, in my new, elegant home.

I turned and lazily stretched out my hand to pull the shade up. It jumped up with a whirr...and soon was out of reach.

Now the room was flooded with bright light. All my bones ached—I was charley horse from yesterday's train, plane and cab travel. Maybe some stretching would do the trick. Nothing felt comfortable—my covers were new and stiff, my sheet seemed freshly starched. Back home Malky and I had slept on bunk beds, and I used to kick my foot up to punch her off the top berth. Just the thought of it made me homesick. I lifted my foot experimentally, but all I kicked was air.

The battered wristwatch on my arm read 7:20, and I felt a strange emptiness and disorientation. I washed *negel vasser* and said *Modeh Ani*, including a special little *tefillah* that things would go right for me in my new life. Then I jumped out of bed and raced to brush my teeth. There was a hairbrush ready and I smoothed out my curls. Now, if I only could remember where I had left my clothes....

I surveyed yesterday's blouse and skirt lying in a heap, soiled and matted. No way I could wear that. If only I could remember where my suitcase was....

Panic engulfed me as I realized that my suitcase was downstairs. Now what would I do?

In an instant it struck me that I could call for help on the intercom. I pushed the button marked kitchen, and called "Susan? Are you there, Susan? I can't find my clothes. Can you please come and bring up my suitcase!"

I heard silence, then a babble of voices all at once. Finally, someone replied, "Coming right up." I waited a few seconds, then heard brisk footsteps from the landing. I saw a smartly uniformed Jenny, wearing a pleated skirt and white blouse. I was embarrassed that she was to be the one to help me.

"Good morning, Leah. Did you sleep well?" she asked, without any real interest.

"Fine, *boruch Hashem*," I replied. "I can't find my clothes! I think I left my suitcase downstairs. Could you please bring it upstairs?" I asked politely.

"You should have been dressed half an hour ago. We're all waiting for you at breakfast," Jenny said a little impatiently.

"Nobody told me when to wake up," I protested, feeling embarrassed.

"In this house we wake up at seven, when an alarm is buzzed into the intercom. You must have slept through it."

"Oh."

"Can I have my own clothes?" I asked. Jenny gave me a funny look.

"We didn't think you'd want them anymore. Take a look in the closet. Mrs. Stein bought you a really lovely new wardrobe."

The way she said it I felt like a neb, a cast-off, a charity case. Who needed their favors? Why would they assume my old clothes weren't good enough? Oh, why did I have to get myself into this predicament! Why did I have to make Uncle Michael's life so difficult that he sent me away?

Jenny had stalked over to the large walk-in closet. Funny, I hadn't thought to inspect it myself.

Wow! It was filled with clothing, all neatly hung

on hangers and folded on the shelves. I stood there and stared.

Jenny knew just what to do. She appraised the row of dresses and pulled one out.

"This is one of your school outfits," she said, even before I saw what she was holding.

Oh, school. Since leaving Uncle Michael's I hadn't had a chance to even think about it, because so much else had been going on. With a start I realized that I was starting my new school today! Now I wondered what my new classmates would be like. For that matter, which school would I be going to?

Jenny stood there, holding the ensemble, wearing a bemused expression. Gingerly, I took it from her hand.

"Is this what I'll be wearing to school? Is it a uniform?" I surveyed the plaid skirt and navy blue cashmere top with distaste. It looked far too elegant and mature, and I would be always afraid of messing it up.

"There are no uniforms at Bais Yaakov High," Jenny informed me. "Mrs. Stein selected these outfits for their style and quality. I hope they fit you right. You're a teen's size twelve, aren't you?"

I nodded unhappily.

"Why am I going to high school? I'm only in seventh grade," I wondered.

"High school begins with grade seven here," Jenny informed me tersely. "They don't have a middle school."

"Oh."

"It is almost a quarter of eight! Please make sure you are downstairs in ten minutes," Jenny said, in a tone that brooked no discussion.

I crumpled up the skirt and made a face at it. Then I straightened it out and put it on. In the closet I found a blue headband to match my outfit, and a full length mirror in which to admire the effect. The navy blue plaid went well with my unruly red hair, and the cashmere sweater was soft and graceful. Not bad, I thought to myself. Still, I didn't feel comfortable wearing these clothes. They weren't me. Luckily, I still had my dirty sneakers—they were the only 'old' thing I wore.

Exactly ten minutes later, I tiptoed down the stairs, marveling at how much more elegant the house looked with the sunlight streaming through the skylight. The heavy beautiful drapes were pulled back from high windows, showing a generous backyard with lots of lawn furniture and a couple of large shade trees, now almost bare. As I walked toward the kitchen, I became aware of how hungry—and nervous—I really was.

All heads turned as I walked in. Aunt Beth and Uncle Gerald were seated at the table reading the newspaper, with Susan hovering near the serving area and Jenny now wiping down the counters. I stood hesitantly, smiling shyly.

"Good morning, Leah," said Aunt Beth. "How was your sleep?"

"Excellent, *boruch Hashem*," I said. "Sorry I overslept."

"Oh, that's okay," said Uncle Gerald. "I'm sure you were tired from your trip. We saved your breakfast for you."

"Thank you."

"Now, why don't you wash and join us?"

I went to wash and then took my place at the elegantly set table, (china for breakfast on weekdays?) made *hamotzi* and took a bite of fresh bread, swallowed, and waited to be served. I toyed with my silverware, admiring the intricate design on the tablecloth and the way everything matched. There was a cloth napkin that I guessed I had to put on my lap. I sensed my uncle and aunt observing me, enjoying my reaction.

Susan came from the stove with a tray of sizzling scrambled eggs, laced with plenty of butter. There was a steaming bowl of farina in the center of the table, which smelled pretty good, but I didn't want to eat so much in front of them quite yet.

The meal was an uncomfortable experience, as I felt Aunt Beth discreetly observing me as I lifted every spoonful of egg and bread into my mouth. Again I tried to eat as politely as I could. She watched me wipe my hands with a napkin and pour myself a glass of milk without any of it spilling.

Then I sipped it as carefully and slowly as I could and wiped my hands once more.

Finally, the meal was over.

"You'll be going to Bais Yaakov High," Aunt Beth informed me. She spoke in a decisive manner, as if nothing I said would count. I felt defeated.

"W...what kind of school is it?" I asked, my voice quavering.

"Don't worry about it, Leah," my uncle smiled. "It's the best high school in town, the highest learning standards, the greatest curriculum.

"I'm a close friend of the principal at Bais Yaakov," my aunt said, "and she's thrilled to have you join the school. I told her you're a bright girl, as we heard from your aunt. Of course, we've hired a tutor to help you catch up, because it is almost three months into the school year."

Hmm...that's interesting. I felt like a pawn on a chess board, with a player plotting my every move. Some of my icy attitude must have gotten through to them.

"Leah, aren't you excited about starting a new school?" my uncle probed.

I shrugged. "How should I know? I haven't been there yet," I pointed out, without thinking. Aunt Beth didn't look too thrilled with that last comment, but she didn't say anything.

"Anyway, the principal is expecting you at nine," Uncle Gerald informed me, breaking the awkward silence. "Beth will accompany you today so that you'll be more comfortable."

The butterflies in my stomach that had slowly calmed down now flew about in full force, making me feel nauseated.

"Yes," I answered slowly, hesitantly. "Yes, I'm ready."

I *benched*, and the Steins bid goodbye to Susan and Jenny, preparing to leave. Uncle Gerald opened the hall closet, picked up a smooth beautiful leather briefcase, and handed it to me.

"These are your school supplies," he informed me. "Beth was running around like crazy trying to get everything right. Oh, and here's your new jacket," he said, pointing to a down pea coat on a hanger. I loved it, but tried not to let it show.

Aunt Beth stood there, waiting for the 'thank you', but I stubbornly said nothing, slipping into my coat. It made an odd contrast with my sneakers.

"Butch is waiting outside to take both of you to school," Uncle Gerald said, opening the front door. I followed the Steins outside and down the staircase, admiring the immaculate wide front yard with its amazing exotic greenery. Aunt Beth and I got into the back of the Town Car without exchanging a word.

The tension was getting to me—a new home, new room, a new school, new friends, all the people at the Steins—so many new things at once! A lump rose in my throat as I thought about my old school and classmates. I hadn't had too many friends there, preferring to stick with my sister, but then again, I had grown up with those girls. What would my new classmates be like? And most importantly, would they like me?

The streets looked magnificent, with wide sidewalks, manicured gardens, lots of different fancy trees. The day was sunny with just a hint of the brisk November breeze of yesterday.

All too soon, Butch pulled up before an impressive stone building with a carved plaque reading "Bais Yaakov High School for Girls."

The double doors were thrown open, and the entrance swarmed with life. Familiar-looking yellow buses emptied; well-dressed girls poured out, talking in groups. Staid older girls with new leather briefcases walked sedately into the entrance. It was much bigger than my school had been.

"Thank you for the ride, Butch," I murmured as I reached for the door.

"I will go with you to the principal," Mrs. Stein informed me.

"Thank you, I appreciate that," was all I said. It was so hard, all this feigned politeness. I couldn't wait to talk to my sister!

Mrs. Stein walked into the building ahead of me. She was so confident and seemed to know exactly where she was going.

I followed at her heels. Girls stopped to glance at us, and I felt a hundred eyes on my back. We entered a bustling, modern office where secretaries sat at computer terminals or answered phones.

"Yes, may I help you?"

"I'm Beth Stein, and this is Leah," she said in her polished tone. The secretaries looked at her respectfully; apparently everyone had heard of my aunt.

One elderly secretary smiled at me, revealing a cracked front tooth. Her gray, steel-wool *shaitel* complemented a pair of severe glasses, yet her face radiated sincerity and goodwill. How I wished my aunt were like that! Though Mrs. Stein appeared immaculate and smartly dressed, her severe, no-nonsense manner intimidated me.

We were ushered into the principal's office, and a tall, heavyset woman with a businesslike manner greeted us.

"Welcome to our school, Leah," she said with genuine warmth. "My name is Mrs. Chana Farber, and I'm your Hebrew principal. We have two parallel classes for seventh grade, and I've placed you in a wonderful class which should be perfect for a bright girl like you. Why don't you follow me?"

"Shall I join you?" asked my aunt.

"No, that won't be necessary," the principal assured her. I breathed a silent sigh of relief.

"All right, goodbye then, Leah, and enjoy your

first day of school!" she said trying to be friendly.

"Goodbye," I replied, glad to see her go. She made me so nervous. And I could tell she hated my sneakers. She must've looked at them and scowled fourteen times.

Our footsteps echoed down the long, tiled corridors, now empty except for a lone straggler or two. Somewhere a bell rang, its shrill tone reverberating in my ears.

Mrs. Farber's pace quickened, and I had to run to keep up. Finally, we paused at a door marked 202.

The principal swung it open and went in. I followed shyly behind. Instantly, five rows of students, five abreast, stood up, waiting expectantly.

"Good morning girls. I am pleased to introduce a new student at Bais Yaakov, Leah Berger. I trust you will help make her feel welcome."

The principal nodded to the teacher, a young, friendly-looking woman, and closed the door. I was left alone to face the music.

"Leah there's an empty seat in the third row next to Yocheved," the teacher said. A stylishly dressed blonde girl looked expectantly at me as I stumbled down the aisle. I felt many eyes on me and (I was sure) on my red hair and even my sneakers. This was a fancier school than I expected. It was not a comfortable feeling to realize how much I stood out.

I sat down as unobtrusively as I could, noticing the wide windows looking out onto evergreens, the brand new desks, fresh chalkboard. In my school back home, the floor had been broken, the chalkboard smudgy and the old desks balanced on sometimes tottering legs. What a difference!

I opened my briefcase and removed a new notebook and pen. Soon the teacher had started her lesson and all the other girls were taking notes. The lesson was about *hilchos Shabbos*, the very same *halachos* I had learned at my old Bais Yaakov back home. Only there, I had been the bright student of a class of only thirteen, while here....

She wasn't a professional teacher, I soon decided. Her voice droned on and on, dealing with the superficialities of each idea, and rarely delving deeper. The students stared straight into their notebooks, barely challenging her statements. In fact, the lesson sounded more and more like a well-known lullaby, and I had a hard time stifling a yawn.

My eyelids soon began to droop....

When the bell rang, signaling the end of class, none of the girls got up. No sooner did the teacher walk out then the next one walked in, as if on cue.

The second class was a bit of an improvement.

Mrs. Zenworth really knew her Chumash and was an enthusiastic gesturer. She got to the bottom point of every idea, and the class was swept right into the action. Although it was new material for me, she made it seem like a breeze. My apprehension melted away as my mind excitedly followed Rashi into a maze of intricacies. Finally, we were brought to the triumphant end, and all the surface difficulties snapped into place, just like that!

Forgetting that I was not in my comfortable class back home with familiar friends, I didn't stop to think about what I was going to say.

"Wow!" I exclaimed, my face rapt. "What a conclusion!"

Then I stopped short. The class was eerily quiet. A titter swept through the back row. Even Mrs. Zenworth looked taken aback. I quickly realized that what I had done was really unusual in this class.

—But not only was Mrs. Zenworth a super teacher, I soon found out she was also a super person.

"I see you really enjoyed that last *p'shat*. Maybe you'd like to read the next Rashi for us?"

There she had given me the chance to prove myself, and now it was up to me. With faltering voice and supreme effort I read the words aloud, and the teacher's encouraging eyes coached me along.

"Well done, Leah. Now let us explain...." I sat back, spent but satisfied. Mrs. Zenworth had established me as an intelligent person in my own right.

Maybe now it would be smoother sailing.

The recess bell finally rang. Suddenly shy, I remained in my seat, packing away my notebook with great care. Out of the corner of my eye, I could see the blonde who I had learned was called Yocheved and another girl they called Chany approaching. A few of the others followed, curious about the newcomer.

"Hi, Leah! I'm Chany. Did you just move to New York?"

I nodded. "Uh huh. I only arrived yesterday."

"Where did your family live until now?"

"We lived in a small town in the Midwest. It's about four hours by plane," I informed them.

"Wow!" Chany sounded impressed. "You really lived in the West? Did you see any cowboys?"

I stifled a snicker. "Not exactly. Cowboys live on ranches in the West. We lived in a little town."

Chany looked miffed. "Well, I was never there so how could I have known."

Yocheved quickly changed the subject.

"Are any of your sisters coming to Bais Yaakov also?"

I tried to hide the blush spreading on my freckled face as I replied.

"No, none of...I mean, I don't have any sisters goin...." I let the last word trail off, giving a wrong impression.

"So you're an only girl! Wow, a privileged character!" another girl exclaimed.

It was too late to explain the misunderstanding, so I let it go by. Anyhow, I didn't want them to find out the truth....

"Does your family have any relatives here?" a tall, husky girl asked.

"Yes. I have an aunt and uncle here. They're rich, with an amazingly huge house," I said offhandedly, trying not to boast.

"That's not such a big deal around here," Yocheved responded sarcastically. "You'll find more mansions than houses in this town."

"That's not true!" another girl retorted. "Just because you live in the 'rich' area..."

"Somebody's jealous," a husky girl taunted, coming to Yocheved's rescue.

I couldn't believe my ears. What shallow, frivolous girls!

One by one, the girls slowly drifted away, and their talk shifted to other matters. I stood near my seat, listening to the conversations floating around me, too insecure to open my mouth. I had the strange feeling of being on the outside, looking in, wondering if it was all a dream that would disappear when I woke up. Several times I closed my eyes and opened them quickly. Each time, the scene was the same.

The rest of the day went by in a blur, and all too soon the dismissal bell rang. Jenny had told me to wait outside for Butch, who would be driving the Town Car. I felt insecure as I watched my new classmates board the bus, not wanting to be different from anyone else.

"Bye, Leah. Are you coming with us?" a few of my classmates waved.

"No, thanks. I'm getting a ride today," I said hastily, hoping the bus would pull away before Butch arrived.

It did.

"Hello, Leah," he said, as I got in. "How was your day?"

"Fine, *boruch Hashem*, you know, like a first day," I said. Butch nodded. I had the feeling that he had plenty to say, but was keeping his distance. I hadn't figured him out yet.

The Steins were still at work when I arrived home. Jenny welcomed me and asked about my day.

"Fine, but I'm sooo tired," I replied.

"You may take a nap now, but make sure to be awake in time for supper at eight-fifteen," she said. "If you're hungry, you can come into the kitchen for a snack."

"No, thanks," I said, wanting more than anything to be alone with my thoughts.

My bed looked so inviting. I pulled the covers up around my chin. They felt soothing and comfortable, with none of last night's stiffness.

The late afternoon sunshine beat through my window, sending patterns of light on my maroon coverlet. My fingers traced the square design, and my mind wandered lazily. I wondered about my sister Malky. What was she doing now?

My mind drifted away from all my concerns and failures, and I fell into a deep, satisfying sleep.

It was early evening, and a gloomy dusk pervaded the room when I awoke, refreshed. I jumped out of bed, hoping I hadn't overslept. It was nearly seven. Another hour and a half till supper (what a weird schedule!) and I was famished. I washed up, brushed my hair and went downstairs looking for company.

Jenny was nowhere to be seen, but Susan was puttering in the kitchen.

"Slept well, Miss Leah?" Susan's warm eyes, partly hidden behind her cap, smiled at me. "Here's a little snack for you."

And before I could reply, she shooed me to a kitchen stool and served a scrumptious cheese danish and glass of chocolate milk.

I made a *bracha* and took a bite.

"Thank you, Susan. This danish is delicious!" I exclaimed, my mouth full.

"Leah, it's so easy to be nice to someone as sweet as you. I want you to be happy here. We all want you to be happy."

"Is that really true?" I asked, guardedly.

Susan looked thoughtful.

"Leah, you must understand that Mrs. Stein wants you to like it here. She cares about you and wants you to be happy. It's just a little hard for her to express those feelings. She doesn't have much experience with girls your age, you know."

"I know."

"So wait for her to open up. With time, I'm sure that everything will turn out fine."

I hoped she was right.

"Susan," I said to her, on impulse.

She smiled at me a warm, endearing smile.

"Can I ask you a favor?"

"Sure. What is it?"

"Can you please call me Rina, instead of Leah?"

"Why?"

"Rina is really my first name. Rina Leah Berger. I'm named after two different relatives. Rina was one of my great-aunts, while Leah was my grandmother. Everyone back home insisted on calling me Leah, but I like Rina much better."

"Then Rina it is," said Susan smiling. "Starting from now! I may make a mistake now and then, but you'll correct me."

"Okay," I smiled. We had a deal. Funny how small things can make you feel a lot better.

Soon after my little snack we had dinner and I felt so energized, that I ran upstairs and wrote a letter to Malky.

Tuesday, November 18

Dearest Malky,

How should I begin? So much has happened since we last saw each other! It feels like it was ten years ago! I can't stop thinking of you, especially tonight when everything is quiet, and the only sounds I hear are the occasional car outside and the creak of the staircase as Jenny (that's the housekeeper—I'll tell you more about her some other time) shuts off all the lights and prepares to go to bed.

The Steins are fine, they leave me alone (sort of), I like my school (sort of), and life is just fine and dandy (sort of). How does that sound? I know I'm not fooling you, Malky. You were always able to see straight through my facade. Oh Malky, I miss you so much! Do you miss me too? Please write back soon! A lot depends on your answer!

P.S. Sorry the letter is so short but it's bedtime around here and I need my sleep so I can function tomorrow. In any case, it's the thought that counts.

How are you doing? Tell me about it, every little detail. I love you and I miss you like crazy.

A thousand kisses,

Your one and only sister, Rina.

A New Friend

icky Kor sat in the back row, her head slumped over her notebook, her back arched, forming a curve. Every now and again her eyes focused hopefully on the teacher, as if begging for the fountain of knowledge to pour over into her brain. From where I sat, two seats away, I could make out where the folds of her oversized blouse hung out of her skirt in a vain attempt to flatter her figure. To put it mildly, Ricky was chubby. It was clear that she derived no small pleasure from food, as evidenced by her bulging recess bag and the eagerness with which she invariably attacked it. Poor Ricky! It didn't look like she had much else to interest her.

Two more school days had gone by, and I was finding my new routine enjoyable. Get up in the morning, go to school with Butch (the school bus was scheduled to begin picking me up the following week), while the Steins drove off to work in their car. When I arrived home I usually had a snack and did my homework, or hung around, following Susan around the kitchen as she prepared supper. Twice I spoke to Uncle Michael and Aunt Shifra, and once I tried to dial Malky in London, but I must have gotten the long distance connection wrong, and all I got was a funny beep tone. I was embarrassed to ask Aunt Beth or Jenny to help me, because I didn't want them listening in on my conversation, which was sure to be emotional. Oh, well. The letter would have to suffice.

Dinner time was a formal affair and the Steins were usually busy discussing their business concerns, asking me a quick 'how was your day' and waiting for me to reply. After supper I did some more homework, or indulged in my favorite pastime—daydreaming—before dropping off to sleep. So far, my social life was nonexistent, and I was enjoying the relative boredom. Life at Uncle Michael's place had been so busy, noisy and hectic, now I took advantage of the large amounts of unstructured time to relax.

And school? Okay, I guess. We had four Hebrew teachers, six general studies teachers and lots of subjects. It was a much bigger school than I was used to—with so many students and teachers. I enjoyed the afternoon sessions—stuff like science, geography, history and literature. As for math (yuck) and grammar, these were to be tolerated, at best. The English teacher, a dour woman named Dr. Shane, appreciated my intense interest in learning new vocabulary words and enjoyed enriching my knowledge with tidbits that the small school back home had not provided. People seemed to be more knowledgeable here. It must be the big city being nearby.

The Hebrew curriculum was a bit of a disappointment. Most of the subjects taught, including halacha and Jewish history, I had covered in my old school. As for Chumash, Hebrew grammar and parsha—Mrs. Zenworth's lessons were interesting, but many of the other teachers' lessons were too easy.

Especially the one taught by Mrs. Mandel, the halacha and Jewish holidays' teacher. She would repeat a point so many times that I would tune out after the first or second repetition. So while everyone copied her words into their notebooks, my notebook would be full of doodling—pictures of Malky and Shira or my mother, or of my old home.

Thursday morning, my third day of school.

"And the reason Cheshvan is called Marcheshvan is...." Mrs. Mandel's eyes darted up and down the rows, until they came to rest on....

"Ricky, would you tell us the answer, please?"

"I...uh....um...." Her frightened stammers jolted me out of my musings, as I looked at her pityingly. A picture came into my mind of a frightened rabbit scurrying about looking for nonexistent shelter.

"Ricky, do you know the answer?" Mrs. Mandel asked condescendingly. Without even waiting for a reply, she acknowledged Chany's raised hand.

"Yes, Chany?"

"Because it's a rainy season," she confidently replied.

Mrs. Mandel slowly shook her head. Ricky caught my eye and grinned, relieved that she wasn't the only one who didn't know the answer. I quickly mouthed the answer to her in a whisper, hoping no one would notice.

"Uh....because of the *mabul*..." Ricky spoke up. All heads turned in her direction.

"Very good, Ricky!" Mrs. Mandel sounded genuinely surprised.

The look of gratitude Ricky shot me made me feel both comfortable and uncomfortable at the same time.

Finally, the recess bell rang, and its noise was tempered by the slamming of notebooks. While the classroom erupted in the good-natured noise of everyone suddenly talking at once, I carefully inched my way to Ricky's desk. She was rummaging through her snack.

"Hi! In the mood for company?"

Ricky looked up and smiled. "Uh, thanks for helping me out today. Want some chocolate cake?"

"No, thanks, not really. I ate a big breakfast. Wasn't it great the way we surprised Mrs. Mandel?"

"Yeah! Thanks for giving me the answer. You could've kept it for yourself!" She blushed a bright red.

"What for? What would I do with it? Eat it for dessert?" I said on impulse, eyeing her chocolate cake.

I burst into giggles and she laughed softly, evoking some curious stares. I noticed Yocheved and Chany casting each other surprised glances. They probably didn't think I was the type to bother with someone who seemed as hopeless as Ricky—what would I want with a girl who could barely keep up?

"You know, I was thinking..." I continued after a moment's silence. "How about, you know, studying together for the parsha test?"

Ricky just stared at me, incredulous.

"Well, do you or don't you want to?" I prodded. "I can come to your house or you can come to mine." Actually, I wasn't that sure about the second part of the deal, and hoped her house was okay. I could imagine my aunt turning up her nose at my choice of friends.

"Well...I don't really know if...I mean...I don't really have any notes and...." She said looking embarrassed.

"I don't really have any notes either, because I just came, but I'm supposed to be going to this tutor—"

I stopped short, realizing that Mrs. Stein had scheduled a tutor for this afternoon, (so she crisply informed me at dinner last night and I had better remember to go after school today). I told Ricky I was really sorry, but perhaps we could study together some other time. I hoped she didn't think I regretted my offer.

But no. Her eyes widened in surprise, and a tinge of jealousy.

"*You're* going to a tutor?" she asked, incredulous.

"Well, I told my aunt I didn't want her, but-but..."

"Your aunt?"

I could have bitten my tongue.

"Um...well...my aunt is taking care of the tutor and...because..."

"It's okay. You don't have to tell me if you don't want to. My mother doesn't care about tutors and things like that. The schools keep on calling her down for meetings, but she never goes."

"Meetings about you?"

"Nah, mostly about my sister. She's in the fifth grade at the elementary Bais Yaakov and she has problems reading and writing. But my mother is too busy with the house and stuff and she just sends back a note that the teachers should do whatever they want."

"Ricky, can I ask you a personal question? I mean, you won't mind?"

"It doesn't matter. If it's too personal, I won't answer."

"Ooh, I love that! You're just like me. Anyhow, the question is this. Doesn't your mother think school is important?"

Ricky opened her mouth to answer, but then thought the better of it as she saw Yocheved inch a bit closer, as if she had overheard our conversation. The other girls were not too far away, either. They all looked intensely interested.

"Don't mind these girls...." I reassured her. "They don't mean anything. I think they just want to be friendly."

"Friendly, my foot!" Ricky retorted. "You should have heard them discussing you yesterday. They were trying to decide why your family moved here, and where your father works. I wanted to tell them that it wasn't nice, but when they heard me listening...."

Brring!! The bell abruptly intruded into our conversation and we scrambled for our seats. The day passed quickly, and I walked out of the school with Ricky. We bid each other goodbye at the school gate.

Because I was supposed to remain at school an extra hour with my tutor, we agreed to talk later that night over the phone.

My tutor and I had arranged to meet at the (now empty) teacher's room. I found her at the doorway, looking a bit too eager as she smiled. Miss Feld introduced herself as Miriam. "I graduated last year from seminary and now I'm working in the special education department at Bais Yaakov Elementary," she informed me. She was amazingly beautiful, with blondish hair and the biggest blue eyes I had ever seen.

"Wow! They really have a resource room?" (probably for kids like Ricky).

"Sure. You can't imagine how overcrowded we are. There are so many kids who really need help and are waiting for their turn. We only have four teachers and almost thirty girls, although of course, not all of them come at the same time."

"Wow. I didn't realize there was such a need!" By now I had sat down on one of the comfortable teacher's room chairs, and Miriam sat down next to me, opening a Chumash.

"You bet. How about becoming a resource room teacher when you graduate?"

When I graduate! Oh, sure! I couldn't even think past the next few weeks, let alone the next few years. I looked at Miriam appraisingly, wondering how much of my background she really knew.

"Miriam?"

"Huh?" she looked up from her Chumash, a

question on her face.

"Did my aunt tell you? Uh, I mean..." my voice trailed off.

"All she said was that you had recently moved from a small town, were staying at her home, and needed some brushing up on the basics," she said, rattling off the details as if she was talking about a shopping list. "Oh, and she did mention that you were very smart."

I blushed. "Oh, sure. Tell me about it."

"Oh, no! We've already wasted fifteen minutes getting to know each other," she gasped, looking at her watch. "Let's get moving."

Miriam really knew her stuff; we spent an enjoyable half hour going over the material for the parsha test. I think I did well, even though I hadn't been in school for most of the lessons. I thanked her politely in the car, as Butch drove both of us home.

"So I'll be seeing you next Thursday?" she asked.

"If you think that's necessary," I quickly replied.

"Your aunt seems pretty anxious for you to catch up quickly," Miriam confided. "I think you could manage well either way, but since she's willing to pay for it, you may as well take advantage."

At that moment, a daring thought came to me. What if Ricky joined our sessions? She could use it much more than I, of that I was sure. I leaned over and whispered my idea.

"I know whom you're talking about. Her mother is not very cooperative. It might be a good idea, but I have to ask your aunt for permission first."

"No—please don't. Forget I asked."

"Well, let's drop the idea then. I can't let her join without asking first."

"Sorry I brought it up. See you Thursday."

"Bye."

My aunt was at a business meeting (as usual) and my uncle was also working late (as usual) so the kitchen was rather quiet for the hour or so that I studied with Ricky on the phone. Patiently, I spoon-fed the material into bite size pieces and repeated it over and over again until I felt the walls must have memorized it!

"To whom were you talking before?" Susan asked companionably as I sprawled, exhausted, on the study room recliner. Her hands were sticky and red from tomato sauce, and she wiped them on her apron as she joined me.

"Oh, just—just a friend," I answered, as innocently as I could.

"It sounded more like you were talking to someone much younger than you," she remarked, affably. "You did a good job explaining. Even *I* felt I knew the stuff by heart!"

Good old Susan. I told her of my new friend Ricky. "You see, I think she's sort of lonely...and she needs someone like me who really knows how to study. So I think it'll work out fine. What do you think?"

"I think you're a gem of a girl, Rina!" Susan really tried to remember to call me by my pet name and I loved her for this. "But maybe it's better if you try not to keep the kitchen phone tied up for so long. I'm going to talk to your aunt about installing a phone for you in your room and we'll get an extension for you down here." (The Steins already had three lines, most of them constantly ringing with business-related calls.)

"That would be great!" I gleefully exclaimed. "And can I go to Ricky after school to study sometimes?" I asked, pushing my luck further.

"I don't see why not," Susan slowly replied. "Of course, you'd have to ask Jenny or Mrs. Stein first, you know."

"I know."

At suppertime that evening, Aunt Beth inquired about my tutor. I sat in my seat, fidgeting, playing with my portion of fried fish and tomato sauce, definitely not my favorite food.

"So, how did it go with Miss Feld?" she asked me, daintily balancing a silver plated fork with her manicured fingers. My uncle, absorbed in his supper, smiled in my direction.

"Great," I replied, still chewing on my flounder.

Aunt Beth frowned. "Please swallow before you talk," she said. "Mind your manners."

Whoa! I hadn't expected her to come on that strong. I blushed, extremely uncomfortable with the turn the conversation was taking.

"Beth, don't be too hard on her," her husband admonished. "After all, it takes a while to develop finesse and polish."

I don't know if he meant it in a nice way, but boy, was I insulted. They seemed to insinuate that they plucked me from the garbage dump!

I sat there, cheeks aflame, attempting to formulate some sort of a response. I tried not to cry or run to my room. Luckily, just then, the phone rang, and Jenny picked it up.

"Mr. Stein, it's Harry from Gemtec," she informed him, "about the conference next week."

Mr. Stein mumbled a *bracha acharona*, excused himself from the table, and went to take the call. I remained sitting across from my aunt.

"So what did you learn?" she asked, breaking the silence.

"Parsha. We reviewed for the test," I tersely replied.

"Excellent. It's important that you do well and get the top marks in the class," she crisply informed me. "After all, you have a good head on your shoulders."

Her voice oozed with what I took to be false enthusiasm. I shrugged.

"Leah, I'm sure you're doing great," she prompted me. "In fact, I think I'll call the principal next week to check on your progress. But tonight I have to take care of a client," she mentally consulted her lists. Of course. Leah Berger was just another 'item' on the list, a figurine to be manipulated, surrounded with luxury, given whatever she wanted on a silver platter, as long as she performed.

I excused myself from the dinner table and escaped to my room. I needed time to think.

My room. Decorated with antique furniture, a closet stuffed with unbelievable clothes and shoes, (we had gone shoe shopping on Wednesday, and came home with two really cool new pairs), and pretty soon, I was sure of it, my very own private telephone. I had a weekly allowance, a phone card so I could call the Steins at work whenever I needed to, and their supermarket account number in case I was ever stranded in the vicinity of the grocery (fat chance!) and was hungry. They were even going to get me a credit card in case I needed to buy something. They had remembered everything.

"Don't worry about the price, Leah," Aunt Beth had assured me at the shoe store, where she made me try on the latest in patent leather shoes with platform heels.

"B...but it's too elegant for weekday," I stammered, not wanting to be called a sissy by my classmates.

"What's wrong with being elegant?" she asked, a

trifle impatiently. She was already nervous because she had taken the afternoon off from work and met me after school.

"Well, I don't want my friends to laugh at me," I stammered.

"Nobody's going to laugh at you. They'll admire your good taste," she assured me blithely. End of story. We got the shoes, stopped at the pizza shop for a treat, (with Butch waiting patiently in the car—I still couldn't get used to that!) and then we dropped Aunt Beth off at work. I was curious about their business, but was embarrassed to ask for a tour. Anyhow, Butch had waited long enough, in my opinion.

In any event, that was yesterday, when I felt like a wide-eyed child, agape with wonder at being able to buy anything I wanted—and having lots of new Shabbos shoes and weekday shoes. Previously my mother could only buy my sister and I one pair of new shoes at the beginning of the school year and became extremely nervous if either of us outgrew them during the year. I was astonished to suddenly be part of the privileged few with so much new stuff. And I couldn't get used to never having to wash dishes or set the table or even make a bed.

Today, however, I was not so sure about all this. If I didn't do well in school or even if I wore my beloved sneakers maybe the Steins would get sick of me and send me off to some other family. This dilemma haunted me as I tossed and turned, unable to fall asleep.

A soft knock at the door. "Good night, Leah," Jenny's voice whispered.

"Good night," I replied, disappointed that it was Jenny, not Susan. Since most of my after-school hours were spent in the company of these two women, I had developed an obvious preference for Susan's company, and preferred to spend my time with her in the kitchen. Jenny tried not to show that she was insulted.

"How was your day, Leah?" she would ask, usually getting a perfunctory "*boruch Hashem*" in reply. When Susan would ask, however, my face would light up as I'd launch into a long, detailed account. Jenny also wondered about the "Rina" part. "Is that a nickname?" she wanted to know.

"Uh, sort of," I replied.

Though my thoughts kept me awake for some time, I set my alarm for the crack of dawn, to get some of my other homework done before breakfast. Before I knew it, it was ringing away, the first pale slivers of sunlight filtering through my window. As I sat at the edge of my bed, dangling my feet and balancing my halacha notes, (we had only Hebrew sessions on Friday) I laughed aloud at the incongruity of the scene. If anyone from my old school would have seen me, they wouldn't have believed this was the same, carefree Rina. Not only did I look like such a snob but Mrs. Stein's subtle comments were putting pressure on me to excel.

From the kitchen, the whirr of the mixer and sounds of puttering about floated upward. Susan was probably baking up a storm for Shabbos. Mmm...the heavenly scent of fresh challah wafted straight to my nose. I was hungry.

I stuffed my notes into my briefcase and raced downstairs, resisting the urge to slide down the banister. (Someday, perhaps, when nobody was home.)

"Good morning Rina," Susan greeted me with a smile. "I see you're up early today."

"Uh huh. Set my alarm. Had to study."

"Good for you. Would you like to test my seven-layer meringue cake? I just took it out of the oven."

"Yum!" I licked my lips. "But I have to say my *brachos* first." I said the *birchas haTorah*, with Susan saying *amen*, and then was treated to a feast the likes of which you can't imagine.

"Oh, I see you're eating an early breakfast." Jenny walked in, as usual immaculate and freshly starched, in marked contrast to Susan, whose shirttails were always sticking out of her apron and whose shoe laces were constantly untied. I liked her that way, smiling and round and untidy. She felt like the Bubby I never knew.

"It's a pre-breakfast snack," Susan remarked, winking.

"Well, I hope it doesn't kill Leah's appetite. We eat in fifteen minutes," she reminded me, with maddening precision.

The Steins showed up in the kitchen right before breakfast, looking fastidious; Mrs. Stein's wig was neatly brushed, her face immaculately made-up (as usual). Her husband's tie was askew, and he was wiping his glasses, but he looked up to smile at me with a special 'good morning'.

"The first Shabbos at our home," he said. "Wait until you see how many guests we have."

"Guests? You mean people with nowhere to go?" I naively asked.

Mrs. Stein looked at me as if I had fallen off the moon.

"No, Leah, when Gerald says 'guests' he's referring to our friends and associates. We do lots of entertaining on Shabbos. People from out of town stay with us. I also have many relatives living all over the country, and they come visit."

Oh. So *hachnosas orchim* becomes 'entertaining'. Interesting. Suddenly, I had become homesick. While Uncle Michael and Aunt Shifra did not have much money, they did have a large table, filled to the brim with good, simple food and surrounded by lots of kids and guests. I had quickly forgotten how stifled I felt in their home, how crowded and annoyed at the noise. What wouldn't I give for a small taste of home?

At least Malky's getting that at Aunt Rachel's place, I decided, as I sat down to eat.

"Why are you so serious?" Aunt Beth asked, scrutinizing me. "I hope you're feeling well?"

"I'm fine, *boruch Hashem*," I replied, distracted. "I'm just thinking."

"Thinking?" she arched one eyebrow. "About what?"

Oh, so now it's illegal to think. But don't you want me to be a brilliant, thoughtful person? Make up your mind!

But all I said was, "About my sister, Malky. I miss her so much."

To my surprise, Aunt Beth looked sympathetic. "I'm so sorry we couldn't take you both," she said. "It was just too much for us, given our schedules. As it is, we barely have enough time for you. The business has taken over our lives. Shabbos is the only time we get to breathe, but we usually have lots of guests and it's over before you know it. On Sundays if we don't work—which is rare—I usually go shopping with Gerald. Sometimes we furnish the house or I update my wardrobe. In this business, you've got to dress the part," she reminded me.

I didn't care too much for her values, I thought. Clothing, entertaining, keeping up with fashion, making a good impression on colleagues. What kind of a life was that? It was so different than my simple small town life. Deep down though I knew there was more to her than clothes. She had gone to college and graduate school and had been a teacher of teachers. She was really smart and respected. She just seemed so cold to me.

But I didn't say anything, I just continued chewing my toast.

"I'm sure your sister is happy at your aunt's house," Aunt Beth said. (Although I couldn't believe she cared! If she had, why couldn't she have taken the two of us?!) "Why don't you call her before Shabbos, just to set your mind at ease?"

"Okay," I replied suddenly sorry for my bad thoughts. "Thank you. I'm having a problem with the long distance code. Maybe you can help—"

"Later. After work—or call my secretary Lauren— she can help you." she said tersely, already getting up from the table. "Gerald, we've got to go," she said, tapping her foot impatiently.

"Sure, bye," he said, hanging up the phone and grabbing his attaché case.

I left later, lingering over chocolate milk with Susan while Butch honked his horn impatiently.

"Rina, I wanted to tell you something to put you in a good mood before school. I spoke to Mrs. Stein and told her that you might want to visit a friend after school, and she liked the idea. You can ask her later this afternoon."

"What if she wants to know who my friend is?"

"Well then, tell her. I'm sure the name won't

mean anything to her. She doesn't know all the families in the neighborhood."

"Thank you so much Susan! Have a good day!" I called out, as Butch honked impatiently once more.

"Bye bye."

I was disappointed that Ricky was not in school that day.

"Where's Ricky?" I asked, at recess time.

"Dunno," Chany said shortly, blowing a bubble with the wad of gum in her mouth. The 'in' girls were gathered around her desk, basking in her glow. Those who did not fit around her desk or merit being part of her exalted circle were left to their own devices.

"Actually she's absent quite often, whenever her mother needs her help," Yocheved explained.

"Why, is there anything wrong?" I asked, as innocently as I could.

"I don't want to discuss other people. It's *loshon hora*," Yocheved self-righteously replied. "Besides, I don't know if she wants it to be public knowledge."

"Then I'll ask her myself."

"I wouldn't if I were you," Zissy joined in. "We once tried it. She gets real sensitive when it comes to her family."

"But she spoke to me once already, and she didn't seem at all secretive."

"Well then, do what you want!" Yocheved shrugged as she looked away.

I decided that they were a nice bunch of girls, since they had tried talking to Ricky. Not really overly nasty or cliquish. They had been together at the Bais Yaakov for so many years that they had formed their own united group. I was so obsessed with keeping my personal life to myself, that I was afraid they'd ask me too many personal questions and I wasn't yet prepared to go over my whole messy life story.

Friday afternoon. When I got home, the house was filled with the sounds and smells of Shabbos. I showered, dressed in an amazing pale pink sweater set and a black A-line skirt I had found in my closet, and wore a pair of black shoes to match. I blow dried my hair carefully, stretching my hair in front of the mirror until the unruly curls were at their best, gathered into a neat bow. Then I surveyed myself before the full length mirror. Not bad at all, considering the way I looked before I came. And to think I never cared much about fashion! I looked so old and mature! If only Malky could see me! If only my mother, *zichrona l'vracha*, could see me!

"Leah, you look lovely," Aunt Beth smiled at me, looking tired. She wore a maroon velvet robe and a long, glamorous wig, hardly appropriate attire for supervising in the kitchen, which she was doing. Jenny was busy with the laundry, while a cleaning woman named Sophia, who came in twice a week, washed the bathrooms and the kitchen floor.

"Uh, can I call my sister, Malky, now?" I asked, in a small voice.

"Oh yes! I'm sorry—why don't you program it and then you can call whenever you want," Aunt Beth replied.

I got the number from Aunt Beth's phone book and dialed it, (correctly this time), but the line was busy.

"Try again later," Jenny advised me, seeing how disappointed I was. "How about calling your Aunt Shifra first?"

I did, and her kids were squabbling, vying to get to the phone and exchange a few words with their cousin, whom they missed 'soooo' much. Finally, it was Shira's turn.

"Hi, Shira. How are you?"

"Uh, fine *boruch Hashem*. School's okay. Mrs. Gordon had a baby boy. Tzipora's brother is engaged. My brother Chaim's front tooth fell out." She filled me in on the many details I had missed.

I listened patiently. Though it was less than a week, the going's on at my old home felt like they were light years away.

Uncle Michael and Aunt Shifra wished me well and clucked sympathetically when I told them I still hadn't spoken to Malky.

"Don't worry, Leah, we spoke to her and she sounds fine," they said and then we ended the phone call by saying, "Gut Shabbos."

For the remainder of the afternoon, I hovered near the phone, constantly trying to reach Malky. I even figured out how to program the phone and just pressed "redial" repeatedly. The infuriating busy signal nagged me, robbing me of my peace of mind. What wouldn't I have given to hear my dear sister Malky's cheerful voice on the line, wishing me a *Gut Shabbos*? But it was not to be.

Okay, time to light the candles. I stood stiffly, at attention, as Aunt Beth spread her arms over the four flames, (one for each of us—one for our Boruch, and one for you—she said). Susan and Jenny also lit candles, on a separate, smaller buffet in the living room.

"Gut Shabbos," said Aunt Beth softly, turning to me. In the magical radiance of the Shabbos lights, her face was transformed.

"Gut Shabbos," I replied, smiling shyly. The first Shabbos in my new home had arrived.

Shabbos At The Steins

The meal was a great success. Uncle Gerald wore a starched white shirt and black suit, and his somber fedora lent a solemn air to the table. Aunt Beth's jewels sparkled and gleamed, reflected in the huge crystal chandelier. The guests—two couples, one young, the other middle aged—sat in their seats, talking in subdued tones.

I was introduced to the guests, who seemed to really look me over, making me blush. "This is Leah," said Uncle Gerald. "And these are Chana and Jamie Schwartz (the middle-aged couple) and Laurie and Manny Gerber."

"Glad to meet you," I said, remembering my manners. Aunt Beth beamed.

"She's extremely bright and well-mannered," she said, talking to her guests as if I were invisible.

Uncle Gerald made kiddush, and so did his guests. Then we washed at a conveniently located white marble sink in the dining room and sat down to eat.

We were not disappointed. The meal did justice to our appetites, and Susan was the woman of the hour. The challah was soft and luscious. The salmon swam in lemon sauce, crowned with herbs, and there was plenty of relish for side dishes. It was astonishingly delicious. Everyone ate to their heart's content.

"Where are they from?" I stage whispered to Jenny, who was dressed in a neat, simple Shabbos dress.

"Don't stare," she whispered back, carefully depositing a china bowl filled with golden chicken soup and *kneidel* at my place.

With no answer forthcoming, I turned my attention to my food. Luckily, Aunt Beth and Uncle Gerald were too busy entertaining their guests to pay much attention to me. I glanced at the Gerbers out of the corner of my eye. Laurie smiled back shyly.

The meal passed pleasantly, with *zemiros* and conversation, (mostly about business acquaintances) and a delicious dessert, caramel cake topped with cherry sauce. It would've been okay if only someone close to my age were there.

"Mmm...delicious," said Mr. Schwartz, his chubby jowls bulging. He had already eaten more than his fill.

"Yes, Susan is a wonderful cook," murmured Aunt Beth, ever the polite hostess.

"We're looking for a good cook," Mr. Schwartz's wife, Chana, said, sighing in exasperation. "Dorothy was great, but she left, and since then, I've been unable to find a replacement!"

"Oh, you poor thing," said Aunt Beth sympathetically, as if not having a cook was the worst problem in the world. It felt so strange to have been thrust into this new world. Never mind the people who had a hard time making ends meet and putting food on the table. Here we sat, dining like royalty, without once getting up to serve, and Aunt Beth was feeling sorry for someone who couldn't find a good cook. Give me a break! I couldn't believe my mother had never told me about our wealthy family! We didn't even have money for necessities.

As if reading my thoughts, Laurie turned to me.

"We haven't heard from you all evening," she said. "How are you enjoying school?"

"Oh, great, *boruch Hashem*," I answered, as noncommittally as I could. "The teachers at Bais Yaakov are nice."

"And what about friends?" Jamie Schwartz cut in. "Have you made any yet?"

"Yes, well, sort of. These things take time, you know," I said, embarrassed.

"There's no rush," Aunt Beth reassured me. "She just came on Monday. It takes a while to figure out who the top girls are."

Aha. So the "top" girls were supposed to be my friends. "Top" in what? I wondered.

"Speaking of friends, have you heard that Chaya Sarah and her family are making *aliyah*?" Chana said loudly, changing the conversation. I was relieved to have the talk shift away from my life, my friendships, my adjustment. Having the guests talk about their lives was just fine with me.

The meal ended, the guests benched, and were shown to their rooms. Out of longstanding habit, I began to clear the table, but was stopped by a bemused Aunt Beth.

"Leah, have you forgotten where you are?" she asked. "You don't have to do any housework around here!"

"But why shouldn't I help?" I asked, yawning.

"You can, if you want to, but I think you'd better be going to sleep. It's way past your bedtime. Did you enjoy the guests?" she asked, in a rare moment of confidence.

"Yes, I thought they were interesting. Especially the Schwartzes. They seemed to have a lot to say."

"Jamie Schwartz is an influential customer of ours, with a large account," Aunt Beth replied.

"He's a big attorney and Chana is his new wife. We knew his first wife quite well. Unfortunately they were divorced two years ago."

"She sounded like she knew his friends pretty well," I remarked.

"Yes, but she's not very educated," commented my aunt, turning up her nose. "I don't know why he married her."

I heard a noise in the hallway, and turned to see Mr. Schwartz walking toward the kitchen in search of a drink. Aunt Beth paled, and so did I. I hoped he hadn't heard.

That illustrates what can happen when you speak *loshon hora*, I thought, as I made my way to bed.

The rest of Shabbos was uneventful. On Shabbos morning, we went to shul, a short walk from our home. There were very few kids there—maybe one or two girls my age, and lots of older adults. The ladies were dressed to the hilt. I stood next to Aunt Beth, feeling so small and insignificant in the gigantic *ezras nashim*. At least I had something to do—*daven!* I surreptitiously peeked out of my *siddur*, trying to make eye contact with the girls, but none of them were sitting near me.

Finally, it was time to go home and eat the meal. Blah, blah, blah, more boring conversation.

Aunt Beth was busy entertaining her guests, and I was left to my own devices. There were always refreshments being served, tea, cake and chocolates. I was a lady of leisure, napping and taking a walk outside in the frigid November air. Though Sukkos was only six weeks behind us, already the Chanukah-like weather was making its presence felt.

I wished I had a book to read, something to break the monotony. Although they had a large library, it was mostly *seforim* or books about finance and business. I wondered if there was a local library, where I could borrow some books. I resolved to ask Aunt Beth on Sunday, but I never got the chance.

Early Sunday morning, she and Uncle Gerald left for an out-of-town-meeting.

"We're so sorry we can't take you along," she said on Motzei Shabbos, "but it's going to be a long day. We also have to take care of some urgent purchases that can't be put off. I'm sorry. I was looking forward to spending the day with you. Susan will be off tomorrow; Jenny was off last Sunday," she continued. "So you'll have Jenny all to yourself."

"It's okay," I said, and meant it. Even sitting around and klutzing all day was better than being entertained by my aunt!

The first thing I did on Sunday morning was call my sister Malky. With barely suppressed excitement, I dialed.

It rang a few times. "Hello?"

"Hello? Can I speak to Malky?" I said, my words

tumbling over each other in eagerness.

"Who's calling please?" the voice sounded like it belonged to my aunt.

"Aunt Rachel? It's me, Leah."

"Leah? How are you?" she said, her warmth making her voice seem so close. "I haven't spoken to you in ages. How have you settled?"

"Great, *boruch Hashem*," I said, trying to be polite. After all, it wasn't her fault that she couldn't afford to give both of us a home. Still, I couldn't help feeling a little angry at her.

"Have you adjusted well? How are the Steins treating you? How's school? Your friends?" she fired off the questions, stopping long enough to hear my "*boruch Hashems*".

"Where's Malky?" I asked, as soon as it was reasonably polite to finish talking to her.

"Oh, Malky's not home," she replied. "She's staying late at school, working at some project."

"School? She has school on Sunday?" I asked, amazed and disappointed that I still couldn't talk with her.

"Yes, but normally she's home already, it's almost two o'clock." I glanced at the clock on the wall, which read ten o' clock, five hours behind London.

"But I wanted to talk to her," I protested, blinking away tears. "I tried calling her all Friday, but your phone was busy."

"It was? I'm so sorry. You see, we don't have call waiting, and Uncle David was on the phone with his parents. Then we took the phone off the hook for Shabbos."

Aha, so I tried to call them all afternoon, forgetting that it was Shabbos already in London! Mystery solved.

"Can you tell Malky to call me when she gets in?" I carefully asked. "I'll leave you my number."

"Uh, I think it's better that you call," Aunt Rachel replied quickly. "Try again in two hours."

I put down the phone, seething. How stingy can you get? Couldn't they afford the price of a phone call? Wasn't it important enough to her, that Malky speak to her only sister? My anger didn't let me see straight and realize that yes, Uncle David was not well-off, and the Steins could certainly afford the call. In my rage, I naively decided to let Malky wait. If she really wanted to talk to me, she'd find a way to call. I wouldn't make the next move, I thought stubbornly, though I yearned to speak to her.

Though I realized how foolishly I was acting, I didn't break my self-imposed stubbornness all through the long afternoon.

The day passed slowly. I wandered around the large house, exploring every nook and cranny. There were four floors in all, (minus the attic). The basement had been turned into a large wood-pan-eled game room and equally airy laundry room, where Jenny did the ironing. On the main level, there was the enormous kitchen, vast dining area and living room, wood-paneled study and den. Upstairs were the bedrooms, and Susan and Jenny slept on the third floor. I amused myself in the basement, playing games on the Stein's fancy computer. When my eyes began to itch, I wandered upstairs, to a silent house. Jenny was probably upstairs.

Now what? The kitchen was empty, and there was no food in sight. I opened the refrigerator—which was packed and found a shiny red apple. Nibbling, I wandered into the den, adjacent to Uncle Gerald's private study. An antique end table stood at one corner, and the couches and loveseats matched the pattern. There was a dainty desk in the corner which I had never paid attention to before. Now I opened the first drawer, and found an old, faded photo album.

Hmm...this might be interesting. Without thinking, I flipped it open, and found myself staring at Aunt Beth, only she must have been ten years younger. She looked so energetic, so vibrant, as she smiled into the camera. Was she really once so friendly? I couldn't believe it.

I turned the pages. There was Uncle Gerald, looking somber and dignified, yet definitely younger and full of life. Though he didn't smile, there was a twinkle in his eye that was hard to miss. And that must be their son, Boruch. He looked just like his father. Hey wait, who's this? I stared at the picture—a miniature version of Aunt Beth, in a five-year-old girl. Was this my aunt? It couldn't be. They didn't have color pictures when she was younger. No, it definitely was not Aunt Beth. Here's another picture with Aunt Beth holding the girl. Who is she? A niece? Another relative? Should I ask?

Suddenly I heard footsteps in the hallway. My heart began thumping. I quickly stashed the album back in the drawer and dashed out of the den, not a moment too soon.

"Leah, is that you?" Jenny asked. "I thought I heard someone in the den."

"Oh, I was just looking for a piece of paper," I fibbed. "I want to do my homework." I didn't think I was not allowed to go exploring but I felt guilty nevertheless.

"School supplies are in the basement," she replied crisply, firmly shutting the door to the den. I was relieved not to have been caught. But the image on the picture would not leave my mind.

I spent the rest of the day pacing the halls, writing in my notebook, and in general, making such a nuisance of myself that Susan, who had come back from her day off towards evening, scolded me to go out and do something worthwhile. "If you want to be productive, you can go to the supermarket with my shopping list," she said.

"I don't know if Mrs. Stein will approve," Jenny

spoke up in an authoritative voice.

"I'm going anyway," I said, stubbornly setting my chin. "I've had enough of klutzing."

"No, you're not," said Jenny. "It's almost dark and you don't know the way. The Steins will be home in an hour and will panic if you're not back."

I reluctantly conceded, hanging up my coat and trudging to my room. I was ready for a good cry.

Dear Malky,

I've been crying, as you can tell by the smudges on my letter. Fool that I was, I spent the day waiting for you to call, furious at the world. Don't you care about me, your only sister? You're my only friend, you know! Why haven't I received your letter? Are you so happy that you've already forgotten about the only member of the family you have left? (Here I really piled on the guilt!)

It's not fair, it's just not fair. School is the dumps, the Steins are creeps, life is so boring. I'm so lonely. I miss you so much. Why am I stuck in this big, empty house, all alone with ticking clocks keeping me company while you enjoy our London cousins?

I'm sending this letter tomorrow, Monday. This is the second one I've written since I arrived. Please write back as soon as you get it.

Longing to hear from you,

Rina

I mailed the letter on Monday morning. That same day, my first letter from Malky arrived. I found it waiting on the kitchen table, unopened, when I came home from school. I ripped it open eagerly, escaped to my room, closed the door, sprawled on my bed, and read.

Dearest Rina,

I got your letter yesterday, and the minute I read it I asked Aunt Rachel for an envelope and stamps. Then I tried to find a nice, quiet place (without any kids around) to write. Hard job. Finally, I chose the broom closet, under the basement stairs. Pretty dusty.

How's life in that big, fancy house? Have you forgotten about me, your one and only sister? I hope not. How am I? Don't even ask. I'm not fine, boruch Hashem. Not at all. I hate it here! I want to go back to Aunt Shifra and Uncle Michael. At least there I had someone to speak to (you), someone who understands me. Here I have no one.

The weather is awful. It's so rainy and foggy. I hate fog! I hate trolleys, the long narrow lanes, the slow moving people on the streets. London, ugh! Tante Rachel's kids are forever barging into the room I'm sharing with Miriam, and Tante Rachel wants to know why my pillow is wet every morning. I'll tell you why, in case you're interested. It's because I

*cry myself to sleep every night. The girls in
school are nice enough, but I can feel their pity-
ing glances. They probably wonder why I walk
to school with my little cousins every day, or
why I never talk about my family. And they just
keep calling me "the American" and making fun
of everything I say. It's like I speak a different
language. You know what a car trunk is?? A
boot. An eraser is called a rubber. Everything I
say makes everyone fall over laughing! Anyhow, writing this letter put me in such a bad
mood that I can't even finish it!*

Love, your forgotten sister,

Malky

One hour and ten tissues later, I tiptoed downstairs. It was quiet in the kitchen; Susan had finished preparing supper. She was nowhere in sight.
Apparently, the Steins were still not home from
work. I hadn't seen them since Motzei Shabbos. No
I didn't miss them especially. There were more
important things on my mind.

I had a phone call to make.

The long distance connection was bad. Static
traveled through the wires. I waited with baited
breath while the phone rang.

"Hellaaaw?" a high pitched childish voice
shrieked.

"Is Malky Berger there?"

"Who is it? Mommy, an American is calling!" her

high pitched voice vibrated into the telephone. I groaned inwardly, waiting for Tante Rachel to come to the phone.

"Hello? Who's—Leah is that you?" her voice rose in excitement.

"How nice to hear your voice! How's everything?" I dutifully answered her questions, but there was really nothing to say. I had already spoken to her on Sunday.

"Where's Malky?" I asked, a trifle impatient.

"Oh, Malky? Wait—I think she's up in her room, reading. That's what she does most of the evening anyway."

As she ran to call Malky, I listened to the lively chatter of the kids, and I sympathized with my sister. Malky loved her privacy, and was unaccustomed to living amidst a bunch of little girls and boys. Even though there was one girl her age, it seems they didn't quite get along. I could have fit in better at Tante Rachel's than she. It sounded like she was really forgotten over there, just one more mouth to feed. Oh, well. It was too late now, anyway.

"Rina?" she softly whispered, and I could tell that she was so emotional she was beginning to cry. "Is that really you?"

"Uh, huh, you guessed it!" My voice began to crack as soon as I heard Malky's voice on the line. I had known that I missed her, but hadn't realized just how much.

"Wait a sec, while I take the telephone into the closet." The noise of kids screaming around her grew progressively dimmer and then I heard the closing of a door.

"I'm here now, in the broom closet. Aunt Rachel will be so angry that I'm twisting the wire, but I just need to talk. Oh, Rina! Did you get my letter?"

"Yes, and as soon as I put it down I dialed your number. Are you really so miserable, Malky?" It was silent for a moment. Then, a sob traveled through the wires.

"Oh, Malky. Don't. I can't bear to hear you cry. Why didn't you tell me sooner? Why didn't you call?"

"Couldn't," said Malky shortly. "Tante Rachel says it costs too much money. They are very stingy over here. I can only take a five minute shower, twice a week, and I have to ask permission first."

"Yuck!" I said, quickly, without thinking. "How can you survive? You know what, if you want to take a shower, come here to the Steins. I've got an entire house to myself most of the time anyway."

"I wish I could join you," Malky said. "But Tante Rachel said that she would never allow me to go to the Steins, and that the only reason you were sent was because there was no choice. As soon as they find another place, I overheard her saying to Aunt Shifra, they plan to send you somewhere else. I wonder if they'll try to squeeze you into their tiny house in London."

"Thanks, but no thanks," I replied, surprised by what Malky was saying. "Five minute showers? I prefer to stay where I am."

"Without me?" said Malky, sounding hurt.

"No, of course not," I replied. "I'd rather be with you than anywhere else. But I don't think Tante Rachel's or Aunt Shifra's is the right place for us. Don't get me wrong. I'm not so happy here either, but at least I've got plenty of room."

"I'm so jealous of you," Malky hiccuped, crying softly. "But I'll never, never even be allowed to come visit you! Uncle David always says he has no money. If you thought Aunt Shifra and Uncle Michael were really poor, wait till you hear what they give us to eat over here! We never even eat any meat—just chicken and too much fish!"

"Oh, you poor thing," I said, feeling sorry for Malky. "Are you sure they won't let you come and join me?"

"Nothing doing. Aunt Shifra and Tante Rachel both hate Mrs. Stein and I have no idea why."

"It's a big mystery, I guess!" I replied. We both were silent for a few minutes, thinking.

"Malky?" I broke the silence.

"Yes?" The silence stretched, engulfing us in its quality. We wallowed together in our shared situation, two sisters separated by thousands of miles and the huge Atlantic ocean.

"Tell me everything!" I ordered abruptly.

And she did. About Tante Rachel and how nice she tried to be, but how domineering it came out. About the kids who didn't give her a minute to herself, and about Uncle David who constantly hinted that she should help Tante Rachel more, and tried to make small talk. About the girls in her class who were ever so polite, but kept their distance from Malky, whom they considered a strange, quiet girl with a funny accent. How everything she did in school seemed wrong and different and how the British girls just laughed at her all the time. About her loneliness, and the way she recorded all her feelings in her diary.

Malky spoke, and I listened.

Finally, when she had her fill of talking and sobbing into the phone, she came up for air. "Tell me all about the Steins, and the school, and...everything."

We talked for a long time, encouraging each other, and sharing memories of our old home. Warmth and hope flowed through the wires, and I felt a soothing contentment.

"goodbye, Malky dear. I want you to say goodbye with a bright smile on your face, even though I can't see it," I teased.

"Goooood night!" she sang into the wires, and I pictured her clear, pale skin glowing from the warmth of her smile.

When I hung up the phone, I washed my face and stretched. It felt so good, talking to my sister Malky. *Nebach*! I had no idea she was so miserable. And I thought that I was miserable. In a way, we both were to be pitied. Two homeless, motherless girls, separated on two continents, one in a rich, empty house, the other in a poor, crowded one. Who was worse off?

"Both of us," I said to myself. Deep down I knew I was being unreasonable, that the Steins were trying their best, but I quickly pushed these thoughts away. It was more satisfying to feel sorry for myself.

No, I wasn't going through what Malky was, but I was so lonely. I longed to have Malky here. But my two aunts wouldn't hear of it. What in the world, I wondered, did they have against the Steins?

I heard voices outside, and the slamming of a car door. Almost instantly, both Jenny and Susan came running down the stairs. They had probably been reading or talking on the phone in their rooms.

The Steins walked through the door, looking exhausted. Aunt Beth smiled at me. "Hello, Leah, how was your Sunday? We missed you," she said, as Jenny helped her with her briefcase.

"Horrible. It was so boring. I klutzed all day. I had nothing to read and Jenny didn't let me go to the supermarket."

"Jenny was right!" said Aunt Beth, sniffing. "You've never been there before. What if you'd have gotten lost? I'd never have forgiven myself."

Jenny flashed me a triumphant look. I didn't meet her eye.

"But I'm old enough to go out on my own! I used to always go shopping for Aunt Shifra!" I said. "It's so boring for me here, all alone in this big house."

Aunt Beth was instantly contrite. "I didn't realize," she said, taking off her coat and hanging it up. "I forgot to ask you. Do you have any hobbies? Would you like music lessons?"

"I love to read," I replied. "Is there a library in the area?"

"We have a library in our home, in my study," said my uncle. "Have you seen it already?"

"Yes, but the books are so long and historical," I replied. "I want to read something more up-to-date, something current."

"Novels are a waste of time," said Aunt Beth flatly, looking in the mirror and smoothing her *shaitel.* "They take your mind away from you lessons. Let's think of something else you can do," she said, as if to distract a whining child. "Do you have any friends you'd like to visit?"

"Yes," I said, jumping at the opportunity. "Her name's Ricky. Ricky Kor. She lives on Blair Lane. Can I go to her house straight from school?"

"I don't see why not," said my aunt carefully. "Just give Butch the address and tell him when to pick you up. He won't be taking you to school tomorrow; hopefully, the school bus will show up as promised."

Uncle Gerald had gone off to his study, but joined us now. "Supper's ready," he said. "Anyone hungry?"

We went into the dinette to eat.

Tuesday morning before I left for school, I gave Butch the address I had written down last week and went outside to wait for my bus.

Ricky was at her usual place in school, and I immediately went over to her desk. "Hi Ricky! I missed you on Friday!" I said a little too eagerly. "How come you were absent?"

"Uh, Um, my mother wasn't feeling well," she replied, "and I had to help. She got better over Shabbos and she let me come to school today."

"*Boruch Hashem.* Do you want to study with me tonight?"

"Um....well...I have to see if my mother lets."

"Maybe if you called her at recess time you could get her to agree?"

Soon it was all arranged. I had a friend! I would go to her home, and be like a teacher—I wanted to obliterate the "dummy" image Ricky portrayed to the world. This would be my special experiment. Starring Rina Berger as world-renowned psychoanalyst and teacher.

It was with no small measure of excitement that I looked forward to dismissal.

But the world-renowned psychoanalyst experienced no minor shock when the school bus deposited us both at Ricky's front door. I mean, I had expected the neglected front lawn with overgrown weeds and the sagging living room furniture. What I didn't expect to find was so many miniature Rickys—coloring at the table, fighting under the table, playing hide-and-go-seek behind the couch and eating snacks in the bedrooms.

"Rickeee...come help me color this picture!" a chubby little boy of about five or six clamored.

"Not now. Now I have to study. Where's Mommy?"

"Hey, dat's your friend? How comes she has such big eyes?"

"Wow! Your hair is so red!" exclaimed another sister admiringly, pulling my curls. Ricky shook her fist at them threateningly.

"Stop that now! This is my guest and I'm taking her to my room and—"

"No you're not! I need to do homework there."

"You'll do homework later. I need some peace and quiet."

"Not fair! It's our room too!" Another little boy stood at the entrance to her room, barring the doorway.

"Mommmmyyyy...." Ricky finally raised her voice in helplessness and exasperation.

A tired sounding voice emanated from the

kitchen. "I'm busy now, Ricky. Can't you watch them for a few minutes while—"

Ricky interrupted. "But I have a friend here. And I want to study."

"Studying is not as important as helping a mother. Tell your friend that you're busy and she can come back another time."

"Can't you tell one of your sisters to take over while you study?" I pointed out.

"Which one? The one who pulled your hair?" Ricky joked wryly. "I get a double portion, 'cause I'm the oldest of nine children. Anyhow, let's go into my room and try to ignore the racket."

I perched at the edge of a disheveled bed and tried to focus on my studies amidst the general clutter. The door kept on opening and closing, as more sisters and brothers wanted to join. They sat in a semicircle on the floor around us, while I repeated the *dinim* over and over again until Ricky could repeat them as well as I. It sounded like a magical spell had been cast over the children, who sat like little angels.

"Oohh...you're such a good teacher!" exclaimed the seven-year-old, who I discovered was named Pesha.

"I wish you were my *morah*—" another little girl joined in.

"Let's hear compliments from the rest," I joked, pointing to Ricky.

"I...I don't know if I ever knew it so well before," Ricky marveled. "You really helped me concentrate!"

"Well, it's not so easy to concentrate in this house, but if you really try to block out all the noise, then you'll succeed. And I can help you."

"That's what my teacher says," the one who pulled my hair confessed. "She always talks to me in private and tells me that even though I live in a noisy house, it's up to me to ignore the noise and study."

"Is that what she says?" Ricky asked, annoyed. "Why doesn't she just mind her own business?"

"I dunno," shrugged her sister. "I'm just telling you what she said, that's all...."

"You know what my rebbe told me? When those kids called me L.D. he said it's not true and I shouldn't care."

"L. what?" I asked, surprised.

"L.D.," Ricky sighed. "It's because of Bina." She pointed to one of her sisters. "Everybody thinks it's contagious."

"What's contagious?"

"Her learning disability. Moishy's friends found out about it from their sisters, and since then...."

"They write L.D. on my desk and make fun of me," Moishy complained. "And all because of you." He stuck out his tongue at his sister. Immediately tears gathered in the corners of her eyes.

"Stop that, Moishy! It's not her fault!" I admonished. "In fact, some of the greatest tzaddikim also had a hard time with their learning. Even Rabbi Akiva, one of the greatest of all tzaddikim, didn't start learning till he was forty! Right, Bina?" I asked, encouragingly.

She nodded, sniffling. I put my arms around her. The other kids looked on, jealously.

"Hey, that's not fair. Bina always gets special attention 'cause she's L.D. I wanna be L.D. too!" Pesha complained.

"You don't really want that, do you?" I asked. She shook her head "no", sheepishly. "Better thank Hashem for your *kepele*," I said, patting her soft brown hair.

"What about me?" the other kids clamored. I marveled at how they all seemed starved for attention. Only Ricky seemed like her mind was miles away.

"Okay, Ricky. Gotta go." I glanced at my watch. "My ride will be here in exactly five minutes."

"No...stay here! Stay here!" five petulant voices surrounded me.

"Kids! Stop nudging! If you nudge her she won't want to come again," Ricky warned.

"But of course I'll come again," I reassured them. "Wouldn't you all like that?" The kids all nodded.

"And Bina, would you like me to study with you too?" I asked, on impulse.

Bina shrugged shyly.

"If she doesn't wanna you can study with me," Moishy offered generously. "Wanna see where we're holding?" And he raced to bring me his siddur.

"I never said I didn't want to." I could barely make out Bina's whisper.

"Then you do want me to study with you. Right?" I asked encouragingly.

"I think you would have to ask my mother first," Ricky notified me. "I mean, if you really want to study with Bina. We had tutors before, and Mommy canceled it because she couldn't afford it."

"Oh, I don't want to take money. *Chas vesholom!* I just figured that if we had time after studying, I could sometimes help Bina.... You know what? Let me ask her myself."

It was difficult getting across to Ricky's mother. She was quite defensive and denied the necessity of tutoring. When she finally agreed, it sounded like she was doing me a favor instead of the other way around.

"But I don't want any problems from her school," she finished off. "If you teach her a different way than her teacher does...."

"Oh, that's not a problem. I can speak to her teacher if you want."

"Are you from the school?" she asked, suddenly suspicious.

"Huh? Oh, no. I'm Ricky's friend."

Permission was grudgingly granted, just as

Butch's horn sounded outside. I rushed into the night, grateful that the darkness prevented him from seeing the squalor that defined their little home. The last thing I need was my aunt finding out the truth about where I went...I just had the feeling that she wouldn't approve.

Mrs. Stein was waiting for me at the doorway when I arrived.

"Did you enjoy yourself at your friend's house, Leah?" Mrs. Stein asked solicitously.

As soon as I saw her, the butterflies in my stomach were activated. "Oh, it was great. We did a lot of studying, and I know the material quite well," I carefully replied.

"That's because I hired the very best tutor to help you catch up," she commented. "You can rely on Miss Feld to help you with all your studying. What is your friend like? Is she as studious as you?"

"Oh, yes. She's extremely friendly and polite. That's why I chose her to be my friend," I fibbed.

My aunt nodded approvingly. "And have you make other friends, too?"

"I'm friendly with all the girls, but I prefer Ricky's company. She always knows the right thing to say."

Mrs. Stein nodded approvingly, as I skipped off with lightheaded footsteps. Ricky had passed inspection!

All that night I rehashed my little adventure in my mind, marveling at how different families were from one another. But I liked Ricky's family—for one thing I had instantly made friends with a whole bunch of kids! In fact, I said to myself as I drifted into a cozy cocoon of sleep, I'd almost rather be in my situation than be born into that family. Maybe I'm not as bad off as Ricky, even though she does have a mother.

A week passed, then another. The gloriously colored leaves were crushed into mulch under our feet, and the days became increasingly colder and shorter. Schoolwork was a gigantic load of studying—and I really looked forward to my weekly tutoring sessions with Miriam Feld.

But as time went on, I found myself one step ahead of my tutor instead of the other way around, and she often remarked that I soon would graduate from needing her services entirely. Of course, she had no idea that her lessons really served a double purpose—because at least twice a week I would go to Ricky's place to help her study. Since I knew the material so well, explaining it was a cinch.

I usually tried to help Bina with her homework as well. Although I didn't have any experience at all with learning disabilities, I found that by breaking down the material into bite-size pieces and simplifying the information, I was able to get through to Bina and make her understand.

Life with the Steins was okay. Soon I got my very own phone and phone number which was really great. The Steins were busy people, and more or less left me alone. They even ate out a few times a week, but when they were home for supper we would exchange bits of news and chat. Soon I didn't feel the same intense stab of longing when I thought of Malky.

I had called her twice since our initial phone call, but was never able to have a long conversation. There was always too much noise in the background on her end and they didn't like her to keep the phone occupied. We promised to write, and I kept meaning to, but schoolwork came first. Malky was also busy with schoolwork, but she loved to write letters. She told me she had sent me a second letter, and I waited for it eagerly.

Finally, one afternoon when I came home from school, I found the letter, postmarked London, sitting on the kitchen table waiting for me. I ripped it open and devoured it eagerly.

Dearest Rina,

Hi! What's up? How's life in the mansion? You want to know about life on my end? Nothing's changed.

Did you know that a baby carriage is a pram? Yossele (that's Tante Rachel's baby) loves to be wheeled in his pram. I take him out in the afternoon, whenever it isn't too rainy and foggy. (Oops, I meant smoggy. Here in London we call it smog, which is a mixture of rain and pollution.)

School's okay, I guess. I mean, how much fun can it be to spend eight hours a day glued to your seat? No, in case you're wondering, I don't have any friends, and am not interested in making any either. There's only one word that describes my classmates: Dumb. They are so babyish, it's pathetic. They still make fun of my American accent. I feel like I'm ten years older than them, but it was the same way in our old Bais Yaakov at home, wasn't it? Do you feel the same way with the girls in your school?

Rina, I miss you tons. I'd give my right hand for you to join me. Come to think of it, you are my right hand. Does that make me your left?

Ha ha!

Love,

Your most beloved sister, Malky, who misses you tons.

P.S. I miss you.

PPS I really miss you.

PPPS I really, really miss you!

I reread the letter for the tenth time, and folded it carefully, smoothing it before reverently putting it away. Reading Malky's handwriting tugged at my heart and made me want to cry.

And to tell the truth, I did.

I felt like calling Malky again. Lately, I called her whenever I felt like it. I rarely used my phone, except to call Malky, and, occasionally, Ricky. I sensed that Malky was jealous that I had my own room, my own bathroom and my own phone. I didn't blame her.

It's funny how quickly one can get used to anything. I quickly got used to never cleaning my room and never clearing up after eating. It became normal the way money flowed freely at the Steins, the amount of clothes I had, the luxurious furnishings that kept on being updated. It all stopped shocking me after a while. I sort of accepted it, but wondered, from time to time—what would my classmates say if they knew the truth about my life?

I considered if they would ever find out. Most of the girls were still pretty unfriendly. If it became known how wealthy the Steins were, would they be friendlier? I didn't care to find out.

I picked up my phone. I had a long distance phone call to place.

The phone rang, as I paced the room nervously, waiting for someone to pick up. Was Malky really so miserable? Just when I was beginning to settle into my new life? I thought of how unfair it was that Malky was still so unhappy!

"Hello?" said a deep voice that sounded like Uncle David.

"Hi, this is Rina Leah from New York."

"Leah! How are you? We miss you so much," he said, effusive and friendly all at once. "Malky never stops talking about you."

"Really?" I replied. "I just got her letter."

"And how's life with the Steins?"

"Fine, *boruch Hashem.*"

"School? Your friends?"

"Just perfect, Uncle David," I replied, sounding like a stranger.

We were quiet for a few seconds, both of us uncomfortable with the conversation's cheery fake tone. Uncle David must have realized I didn't want to share any more details, so he just said, "Okay, then, I guess I'll get Malky. She's probably upstairs, reading, as usual."

I giggled. That was what everyone said whenever I called. Malky spent all her time reading. But then again, she always had.

Soon I heard hurried footsteps and then her breathless voice.

"Hello?"

"Malky! How's life, sis?"

"Rina! You got my letter?"

"Uh huh. Is it really so bad?"

"Worse!" Malky sounded bitter and angry. "I hate everyone. Aunt Rachel, Uncle David, their nosy kids. Sometimes I even hate you. I mean it!"

"You can't be serious, Malky?" I felt suddenly awful. Like I had a big stomach ache.

"Uh huh. You just call me because you want to be nice. But you don't really need me. You have your own room, your own phone, everything you want. And I have nothing! Not even a little quiet place to read! There's not even room for me at the dinner table!"

Could Malky be jealous? Could it be?

"Malky," I said, trying to think of the right words to convince her. "I want you to know one thing. I will always, all my life, love you more than anything. You are the only one in my family I have left," I said, trying to blink back my tears. "How can you say that I don't care about you?"

"I know you care about me, Rina, but sometimes I'm just so angry I can't think straight. I'm angry for Mommy dying and for having no father and for being dumped in different houses. And then I hate everyone."

"I don't blame you, Malky, but I want you to realize something. By being angry at the world, and blaming everyone for your situation, you only hurt yourself."

"Oh, sure. It's easy for you to speak. Come here and see for yourself how mean everyone is to me!"

"Malky, I'm sure it isn't easy for you, but don't think life is so great at the Steins either. I'm getting used to it, but, you know, I still don't love it. I'm always lonely, and I don't have any friends (except Ricky, but I didn't bother mentioning her to Malky), and sometimes after I do my homework I just sit and daydream about how good life was before Mommy passed away."

"Don't! Don't even remind me because I'll start crying again," said Malky.

"So I won't. But I want you to know something. Everyone has a choice. We each can make our own decision, either to be angry and miserable and blame the whole world, or start accepting our situation. No, I don't mean dancing for joy," I said, as Malky started to protest, "But at least we can make an effort to get used to it. I just saw an interesting proverb, someone brought it to school. 'Life is 10% how you make it, and 90% how you take it'."

Malky was silent for a while, and because I know Malky, I knew she was thinking over everything I had said.

"Does that make sense to you, Malky?"

"Y...yes," she admitted crying a little as she spoke, "but it's so hard to be happy when nothing is going right."

"I know Malky. It isn't easy, but it could always be worse. We could have been put into an orphanage, and beaten and starved. We could have been sent to work in a factory! We could have been left to beg on the street in rags..."

"Stop!" said Malky, laughing. My imagination was getting the better of me.

"Okay, but you get the picture. So hang on and keep smiling!"

As I put down the phone, feeling smug and pleased with myself, I had no idea that soon I would

be the one who needed this very piece of advice I
had dispensed so self-righteously.

Trouble Ahead

Jenny was as pesky as a fly. She was always probing into my life, wanting to know why my friends never called.

I usually went straight into the kitchen when I returned home after school—it was cozy and Susan always prepared the best snacks. The only problem was that Jenny and Susan would often hover around me.

"I often hear you speaking on the phone, upstairs," Jenny once commented. "Why do you always call your friends? Don't they ever call you back?"

"Oh, they do," I assured her.

"All I hear is you dialing and then a long, giggly conversation. Do you always speak to the same

157

girl?"

"The same few girls, sort of. Those that are my type."

"Just who is your type, I'd like to know?" she queried. I shrugged my shoulders and pretended to be insulted.

"Susan, is it okay if I'll be late today? I want to go to my friend's to study again—" I called out one day on my way out the door to the bus stop.

"What, another test?" Jenny remarked. I didn't bother answering her.

"You know, Susan...." Jenny started.

I paused at the doorway, ears straining to catch what she was saying. But I couldn't make out one single word.

Luckily, I didn't need too many friends. I had found out about a library at school and was looking forward to borrowing some books to read tonight.

Bookworm that I was, there was almost nothing I enjoyed better than to curl up with a good book. The written words transported me miles away, and I felt like I entered the lives of every character and lived along with them.

I discovered the library by accident during one recess. I was sitting at my desk, so absorbed in my thoughts, that when I suddenly looked around me, I realized that the classroom was almost empty.

Then I remembered that the rest of the girls had gone to the auditorium to watch the eighth graders trying out for the Chanukah choir. The only other person in the room besides me was deeply engrossed in a book.

I glanced up at the same time she did. Our eyes met, and we smiled at each other. Dina was no newcomer to our class; she had been with the same group of girls since first grade. Still, she preferred to read than to socialize, and her comments in class, while few, showed her to be meticulous and studious. While she didn't lack admirers who needed her assistance with their homework, Dina seemed not to need companionship as much as I. Thin, pale-faced and introverted, she appeared to coast through school with ease, never complaining or making anything seem hard.

"What are you reading?" I craned my neck to get a better glimpse.

"It's really a babyish novel, but I love the part where the twin sisters fight. It's called *The Great Confusion*," she added as an afterthought. "Have you read it already?"

"No, but I'd love to. Are you nearly finished?" I asked excitedly.

"I'll be finished in a day or two, and then you can borrow it after me. If you'll come with me to the library, you can get it right after I return it. We just have to watch that the librarian doesn't notice, because she may not allow it. She says it isn't fair."

"Huh?"

"It isn't fair to give your friend the next chance at a book. We have to replace it on the shelves so that everyone can get a turn. There are long waiting lists for the new library books," she patiently explained.

"Which library are you talking about? Is it near-by?" I asked, wondering if my aunt would think it classy to let me join.

"Oh, two classrooms down. I'll show you. Come with me!" She reluctantly put her book down, while I followed at her heels.

"Wow, the school actually has its own library?" I asked in amazement as Dina knocked on the solid door and waited for it to open. "When you men-tioned a library, I thought it was somewhere else in the neighborhood. This is great!"

"The library is years old, almost before Bais Yaakov took over the building. It belonged to some other school, once upon a time."

"Why didn't I hear about it until now?" I asked as the doors swung open. And then, my only comment was "wow!" as I surveyed the massive shelves filled with books.

"Can I help you?" a disinterested voice asked sharply. It came from the room's only occupant, a middle-aged woman with sharp eyes.

"Uh...I'd like to join the library," I stated, nodding goodbye to Dina who had turned to leave.

"Your name please?" I had the feeling that she was presiding over an interrogation.

"Rina Berger."

"Spell that for me, please."

I did, as her spidery handwriting headed a brand new index card. Next, she asked me to fill in my grade and the date. Then I handed it back to her.

"Okay, let me tell you something about the way I run this library. Members pay $15 for the school year, and can take up to three books per week. Every book has a card in the inside pocket, which must be signed and put in a plastic holder. You leave that with me, and when you return the books, I cross your name off that list. If a book is late, you must pay 50 cents for every day you're late."

"Oh, I'm sure I won't be late."

"That's what they all say. And then they come with excuses. 'Oh, I'm so sorry, I had a big test and I forgot.'" her voice mimicked. "But excuses don't faze me. You're late, you pay. And don't you scratch or damage the book, because you have to cover its full value. Some of these books are nearly falling apart, so be careful not to loosen the binding."

"Oh, I know how to take care of books," I assured her. "Besides, we have no small children in the house to ruin them."

"Hmph!" was her only reply. She seemed to be in a bad mood. I wondered what was going on in her mind.

So I became a member of a library for the first time in my life, carefully choosing the books I want-

ed to read. I took a twenty-dollar bill out of my
pocket—it was my allowance for the past two
weeks, (I never needed to use it until now) and paid
for a membership. (It felt good not to have to worry
if I could afford it or not.)

The school day seemed to drag. I couldn't wait to
get home and slip upstairs to my room to deposit
the books in a safe place.

"Good afternoon, Leah. How was your day?"
Jenny asked kindly, scrutinizing my face as I ran
into the house, flushed and disheveled.

"Fine, thank you. Where's Susan?" I asked, not
really aware of how rude I sounded.

"Susan isn't feeling well, and she went to see the
doctor. She has heart problems, you know."

"Oh no! Is she okay? She never mentioned anything!" I said, concerned.

"There are lots of things you don't know about
this house yet," Jenny said sounding almost cheerful. She was in a good mood, for a change.

"How long have you been working here, Jenny?"
I suddenly asked on impulse.

"Just over three years."

"And before that?"

"The Steins had someone else, but they weren't
happy with her."

"But that's not what I meant. What did you do
before you came here?" I persisted.

Her eyes took on a faraway, misty look, and I

sensed a cloud come over them.

"Never mind I asked," I cut in quickly. "It isn't my business anyway."

"That's right. Now, would you like something to eat, or are you going to that special friend today?" she asked sarcastically.

I sensed that she was afraid to open up, as if there were something painful that she was holding back, which made her act sarcastic every time the conversation turned too personal.

"No, not today," I replied. "Can I take an orange from the fridge?"

When Jenny was around, I always hesitated to help myself, although Susan encouraged me to do so.

As soon as I finished the orange, I escaped to my room. The Steins were trying to meet an end-of-year deadline in their business, and lately worked late every day. I didn't miss seeing them at the supper table, and was happy to be left alone.

The evening wore on, but I was oblivious to it all. At Susan's urging, I came downstairs to eat a solitary supper at seven thirty, but barely had patience to finish my meal—I was so excited to finally have something to read!

I spent the evening curled in bed, the reading light shining on the tattered pages of my borrowed book. The only sound I could hear was the tick-tock of my alarm clock. I was in my own dreamland, and immune to interruption. I barely paused at the sound of the Steins' arrival home, nor the regular sounds of the late supper served to them and then cleared. In the dim haze of my consciousness, I was aware of the house quieting down, and the blackness outside my window growing richer and deeper. The pages of my book seemed to turn of their own accord, and finally I reached the last page and closed the book with a satisfied sigh.

My sigh turned to horror when I glanced at my alarm clock. It was nearly one thirty in the morning, and I was still fully dressed! Silent as a feather, I undressed and got ready for bed, then fell between my covers, exhausted.

I overslept the next morning. An annoyed Jenny came to wake me, and I raced into my clothes. Wiping my bleary eyes and stifling my yawns, I ran downstairs to the breakfast table. I was relieved to see Susan back in the kitchen.

Mrs. Stein eyed me suspiciously. "You look tired, Leah," she commented. "Are you feeling okay?"

"Yes, I'm fine. I just had a busy week with studying and tests."

"Jenny, is Leah getting enough rest?" Mrs. Stein asked.

"As far as I can tell, her lights are out at ten thirty. Unless there's a test the next day and I let her study till a quarter to eleven," Jenny replied. Susan winked at me from the stove.

Jenny was so precise!

"Well then, I wouldn't worry about it, Beth," her husband assured her with a smile. "I understand you're doing quite well, Leah, and soon the parent-teachers meeting is coming up. I'm sure you will make us proud!"

I smiled back at him, though for some reason I felt like sticking out my tongue.

I yawned throughout the school day, and then through my tutoring, and finally through my tutoring session at Ricky's house. Bina looked eager to see me, and after studying a half hour with Ricky to make sure she understood all the lessons we learnt that day, I concentrated on Bina. I had a feeling that Ricky felt more comfortable when I focused on teaching Bina. Sure, she appreciated my studying with her, but how must it feel to always be on the receiving end of a relationship?

Yet, while Ricky didn't realize it, she was giving something extremely valuable as well—her genuine, unflinching adoration of me. I had felt so lost in this new place without any family or anybody I even knew. It made me feel strong and good about myself to help others. The poor little orphan girl, nobly giving free lessons.

And I enjoyed having a make-believe little sister like Bina.

I had begun teaching her the ABC's, and we were already up to the letter "P".

"Good girl, Bina. And can you tell me another word that begins with a P?"

"Uh…um…party. And punch."

"Good! Party and punch. Punch and party. We drink punch at the party."

"No, not that punch," she giggled. "Punch, like this. What my brother always does to me."

"Your brother always punches you?" I asked, as I noticed a mischievous grin forming in Yanky's eyes. He was curled up listening, as usual. I suddenly realized that I had made a big mistake, as the carefully planned lesson turned into a brother-sister fighting match.

"Stop that now!" I snapped. "If you don't, I'm going home!" Yanky's fist froze in midair.

"Hey, she looks really angry today," he whispered.

"If I look angry, it's just because I'm tired," I excused myself with another yawn.

"Why are you tired?" he demanded.

"Because I went to sleep late."

"I always go to sleep late and I never get tired!" Bina interrupted.

"Good for you. But I went to sleep really late."

"Why?" they asked eagerly. For them, every answer invited another question.

"Because I was reading a book."

"Why?"

These kids weren't too interested in books. But I

was determined to change this.

That night my aunt ordered me to bed early, and I dutifully climbed into my nightgown as Jenny shut the lights off. But the lure of my two unread books beckoned to me, and I tossed and turned between my covers, unable to fall asleep. The luminous dials of my alarm clock read past midnight when I tiptoed out of bed to check if the house was dark.

Then I cautiously flicked on the lamplight, and fluffed up my pillows. I reached for the book, hidden under my bed, and opened the first page with a satisfied sigh.

Time passed deliciously. At first, I didn't hear the footsteps.

They came closer and closer, then the door was suddenly thrust open.

My heart skipped a beat as I looked up in fear. There were two eyes looking straight at me—eyes blazing in anger. And they belonged to Aunt Beth.

An elegant robe was hastily wrapped around her, and she looked eerie in the dead of night.

Her voice, when she finally found it, came out in sputters.

"So this is what you've been doing the past few days! Wasting your time reading silly stories instead of studying! You could have been at the head of the class by now if you'd study instead of read novels. Look at the clock—it's nearly morning! Staying up late will make you sick and you won't be able to concentrate at school!"

"I...I'm sorry...I didn't mean to wake you.... Was I making any noise?"

"Noise? Noise? You nearly had me doubled over in fright when I saw your light still on at 2:00 a.m. I couldn't imagine what you were still doing!"

"But it can't be 2:00 yet. I haven't been reading that long!"

"Don't make me out to be a liar. Look at the alarm clock and tell me what time it is right now!"

She was working herself into a frenzy, her face flushed and angry. I had never seen this side of her before, and I was frightened.

"It...s...forty-five minutes past one, Aunt Beth."

"Don't 'Aunt Beth' me. And give me those books this minute!" She seized them from my lap, snatching each one with gusto.

"Oh...but they're library books, and they have to be returned tomorrow or they'll be late!" I pleaded, my voice sounding unnatural in the ensuing silence.

"You should have thought of that before you broke the rules in this house. You know very well what time you have to be asleep. I'm confiscating these books and I'll make sure to return them. I'll also be sure to tell the librarian not to lend you books anymore!" she emphasized.

"But I have a library card!" I protested, and then

regretted my words the moment they were uttered.

"Then give that to me too," she insisted. I rummaged through my briefcase, my face suddenly hot. What right had she to barge into my room and confiscate my library card?

"That will be it. Now I will close your lights and from now on your bedtime will be half an hour earlier. You will not put your health at risk while you're in my home! Good night!"

"Good night," I mumbled as she flicked the light off and turned to go. I waited at the door until her footsteps faded away, and there was silence.

Then I tossed and turned in bed all night, wondering what to tell the librarian.

The next day was a nightmare. It began with breakfast, where I had to face her, and actually mumble a good morning. Then, at recess, Dina invited me to accompany her to the library to return her books. I was embarrassed to tell her what had happened, so I mumbled an excuse.

"Leah, the librarian wants to see you," Dina announced upon entering the classroom five minutes later. "It's about your books, I assume."

"Are you sure she meant me?" I asked in consternation.

"Pretty sure. On the other hand, I don't really know. I think she said Rina Berger. Do you have a younger sister here?"

"My other name is Rina," I admitted, as some of

my classmates stopped talking and turned to stare at me.

"Hey, that's cool," said Chany.

"When my sister was a baby, she had a hard time pronouncing Leah, so she called me by my other name, Rina. And it stuck."

"What does your mother call you?" Dina asked curiously.

The bell rang, saving me from the agony of having to explain.

It was too late to go to the library at recess, so I dropped in during lunch hour. I found the librarian sitting alone over a pungent sardine and pickle sandwich. I wrinkled my nose involuntarily.

"Yes, can I help you?"

"Someone told me you asked for me?"

"Your name, please?"

"Rina Berger. Uh...I'm sorry that my books are late. I...uh...I don't have them with me at all...."

"I know all about it. You just got a library card and you're already late! You're just like all the rest. Well, you'll have to pay 50 cents for every overdue book. That's $1.50 for today and $1.50 for every day late."

"But that'll be hundreds of dollars!" I protested, dread welling up inside of me.

"Why, did you lose the books?" she asked, a superior glint appearing at the corner of her eye.

My face turned beet red as I explained my

predicament.

"Aha. Well then, I'll need your aunt to call me. Are you boarding with her this year?"

"Well yes...and no. I...I don't think she'll call. She's quite busy. So...here's the dollar-fifty." Hesitatingly, I handed her the last of my carefully hoarded cash, with which I had planned to buy pizza the next time the school was selling it.

She pursed her lips and put the money in a special folder. Then she turned to me, her expression softening somewhat.

"So she took the books away, eh? Well, I'll have to call her then. Do you have her number at work?"

"N...no," I fibbed.

She looked straight at me. "Don't beat around the bush, Rina. Will you kindly give me her number at work?"

I had no choice but to give it to her, and then she made me wait while she called. I hoped the line would be busy, but I had no such luck.

The conversation was brief and official. There was a little confusion about my name and then the librarian informed her that the fee for overdue books would be continued until they were returned, and that under the circumstances, I could not be a member anymore until the matter was settled.

"Oh, so you don't want her to be a member at all? Very well then, I will refund the library money as soon as the books are returned."

"Thank you for your time."

"Good day to you, too."

The librarian turned to face me, a look of genuine sympathy on her face. "I'm sorry, Rina, but it seems your aunt is not happy about your membership here. She doesn't think it healthy for a young girl to read novels. And don't worry about the books. She said she'll mail them in."

I swallowed quickly, and mumbled, "goodbye then, and thank you." From the look she gave me, I had the feeling she felt sorry for me.

The day dragged on, and I wasn't prepared for the history quiz, nor for the 75% on the math quiz of the day before, when I had been too tired to concentrate. I stared at it grimly, with the funny feeling that I was in deep trouble.

Trouble met me at the front door, where Jenny was waiting with a serious expression on her face. "Good afternoon, Leah. Mrs. Stein would like to meet you in the study. She came home from work early today. Go upstairs and freshen up first."

"Wha...can't she meet me in the kitchen? I'm hungry!" I protested. Jenny did not answer.

I sat across from my aunt, my eyes focusing on her stockings and high heeled pumps. I took a deep breath, waiting for her to begin.

"Look at me, Leah," she said sternly, and I did, expecting the worst.

"You have let me down in the worst manner possible," she began. Wow, could she still be that angry about yesterday, I wondered.

"You have lied to me."

My mind raced in dizzy circles. What could she be talking about?

"Susan told me you were visiting a friend. I called your principal today to discuss the library books and inquire about your progress. Imagine my surprise when she complimented me about the wonderful *chesed* work you were doing. There's nothing wrong with *chesed* work but not when it makes your own grades suffer!"

Uh, oh. Did I know what was coming next! Now I really was in big trouble.

My aunt paused for breath and continued.

"Didn't you think you should ask permission to spend all your spare time with Ricky Kor?" she spat out the name as if it were a disease. "After all the effort I put in to hire a tutor so that you should be at the head of your class, you insisted on sticking to a girl who can barely keep up. Let me see your test results!" she insisted, in fury.

Hands trembling, I reached inside my briefcase, hoping there was nothing there. No luck. The math quiz cringed in my fingers, and I placed it in her outstretched hand, waiting for her to explode.

"So this is the outcome of your new friendship?" she asked in an icy tone.

I had had enough.

"That's not fair! Ricky is a fine, upright and wonderful girl. Is it her fault that her mother can't cope and her sister is learning disabled? Is it her fault that she gets so self-conscious she can't answer any questions correctly? Is it her fault? Is it my fault I don't have a mother?"

I was sobbing by now, the words coming out in short gasps. My aunt looked shocked, like someone had hit her over her head.

"Enough! Enough!" she finally said her voice suddenly gentle. "You will be grounded in your room and I'm afraid there will be no supper for you today until you apologize."

And then she turned and left, leaving me with my pride, pride which didn't let me apologize.

I simmered and stewed for an hour, walking around in circles, my mind full of rage and hurt. I couldn't understand what she had against Ricky? Didn't she realize what really counted in life? She acted like...marks were the basis of one's life, and a girl that did less than average or who was really poor was to be shunned.

After I had cooled down somewhat, I was able to think rationally. I realized that my aunt had nothing against Ricky. She was simply disappointed. She had wanted her niece to be the shining star in the class, not a nameless girl in the back row who spent all her time tutoring someone else.

She had wanted to be invited to school conferences where she would hear glowing reports, not to be told on the phone what a "doll" I was, tutoring some unfortunate student.

Just the same, I wished she would understand. How I wished she would be a bit more like my mother had been—I bet my mother would've been proud of me.

A spasm of longing for my mother took hold of me, and I bit my lips fiercely until I couldn't help it and the tears came of their own accord.

I cried for myself stuck with no mother in a new family. I cried for Malky, safely tucked away at Aunt Rachel's. I cried until I started to hiccup. When I couldn't stand it anymore, I washed my face and tried to put myself together.

Malky. How I missed her. How long was it since I had last spoken to her? It must have been at least a week. I picked up the phone in my room to dial, but then thought better of it. I didn't want the Steins to overhear my conversation, or Aunt Rachel to hear that I had been crying. Instead I took out a piece of stationary and penned a letter to Malky, pouring out all my hurt. As I wrote, I felt better, as if some of the weight of my sadness was being lifted off me. I felt there was someone out there—however far away—who understood.

Two hours later, I was nearly done, when I thought I heard a faint scratching at the door.

"Who is it?" I whispered.

"Shh...sh...let me in!" I nearly jumped for joy when I recognized Susan's voice. She tiptoed in, carrying a steaming tray.

"I'm sorry about what happened. Jenny told me all about it. You poor thing, you must feel awful!" Her sympathy reopened my wounds, as the tears began to flow afresh.

"Now, now, don't you cry, dear. Mrs. Stein won't be angry forever. She'll forgive you. Calm down now, and eat the supper I brought you." She held a steaming tray, which she deposited on my desk.

"I don't need supper," I said, angrily pushing away the tray. "I want to go back to Uncle Michael and Aunt Shifra! I want to go back now!" I added, with stubborn finality.

"Don't be silly, Rina. How would you go? Anyway, until you figure out a way to get home you don't want to starve! So eat to your heart's content, but don't tell anyone that I brought you the food."

I shot Susan a look of pure gratitude.

I had never enjoyed the taste of vegetable soup and breaded chicken more. I ate hastily, with appetite.

"My, that was quick," she approved, standing over me as I finished. "What are you writing there?" Her eyes glanced at my letter, nearly finished.

"N...nothing. Only a letter to my sister in London," I stammered. "Where can I mail it?"

"Why don't you ask Jenny for some air mail

stamps? She's bound to have some in the study. Only, wait a day or two, until this thing is cleared up. Anyway," she continued hurriedly, "gotta go now. Jenny will be missing me. So have a good night and don't be too upset! Everything will work out in the end!"

"Good night, Susan! And thank you so much for the food!"

Feeling much better, I stowed the letter in my briefcase and went off to sleep.

Early the next morning, Jenny informed me that although I was still grounded, I was not allowed to miss even one day of school. I would be permitted to come down for meals, and then Butch would take me to school. That was that.

The letter was still on my mind all the next day, and I read it carefully at recess, while Ricky studied from my notes. I regretted having to tell her that I probably couldn't study with her anymore, but I couldn't bear to disappoint her by abruptly discontinuing the lessons. To my relief, she didn't ask too many questions.

"So, should I tell Bina that you won't be coming anymore?" she asked wistfully.

"Um...I don't know. I think—tell her that I won't be coming this week. After that, we'll play it by ear."

"Okay. And Rina?"

"Yes?"

"We still can be school friends, can't we?"

I nodded, hoping none of the other girls were curious enough to overhear.

Then I turned my attention to the letter I had written to Malky the night before, and I mouthed the words aloud as I read.

Dearest Malky,

How should I begin? Will it be: Hi, how are you? Or how about: How's life treating you over there? I think the second beginning is better. After all, it's been nearly two months since we last saw each other (at the goodbye party where everyone was trying hard to smile with this gigantic lump in their throats!) and wow, do I miss you!

Now, I know that this cheery beginning won't have you fooled, and that though the teardrops will long have dried by the time this letter gets to London, your sharp eyes will notice the smudges and smears. So instead of fibbing about how happy I am, let me say it black-on-white: I am miserable here in this elegant, horrible, evil Stein mansion. I want to go home, to Uncle Michael and Aunt Shifra, or join you at Tante Rachel's!

Don't think I've felt this way since I came here. Oh, no! In fact, I did sound cheerful the last few times I've spoken to you, didn't I? We even had such a nice conversation about being happy. For the past few weeks I've been fluc-

tuating somewhere between "might as well get used to it" and "will I ever get used to it?" Life with the Steins would even have been tolerable, oh, if only you would be here with me! I'm sure you feel the same way.

Let me start by describing where I am now. I am (hold on to your chair) locked into my bedroom, under threat of severe punishment if I dare leave unless I apologize. And you know your sister well, Malky—I have no intention of saying I'm sorry for doing something which I feel was right; so this bedroom will be my haven for a long time. Anyway bedroom is not really the appropriate word to use either— exclusive suite would fit the bill.

Remember the girl's room of our dreams, Malky?? I thought it had finally come true when Susan—you know Susan from the way I described her—introduced me to my new room. From the looks of it, it could have been designed for the president of the United States or the Queen of England—anyone but me!

The huge, oak four poster bed only exaggerates my loneliness on these long, dreary winter nights. My bedtime is 10:00, whether I'm tired or not. It used to be ten thirty, but that was before "It" happened.

"It" all began last week when Dina, someone in my class I hope to be friends with—she's a bookworm like me—introduced me to the school library. Since my social life unfortunately consists of only one friend whom I tutor in my spare time, I jumped at the offer. The librarian warned me to return the books on time, and I was sure it would be no problem. Well, it would have been no problem had I not been so eager to finish the books that I stayed up till 2:00 a.m. to read them, and that is how dear "auntie" found me.

The rest is history. I got into trouble, she called the principal who told her what a "nice little girl" I was for tutoring my classmate (Ricky's her name) as a chesed project and that my grades were okay, but not spectacular. This didn't quite fit with her picture of a classy, well-educated young lady, (I think she never got anything but A's) and I felt the effects of her temper.

I had often wondered, in the good times before Mommy died, what it would feel like to be living somewhere you don't really belong? Well, dear sister, now I wonder no more. I feel like taking the next train back to our sweet little town—if Uncle Michael would want me back. After all, isn't it best that families remain together, no matter the cost?

I have so much more to say, but that would take hours. I'm saving all of my experiences in *my mind for when we speak again. And don't worry. I suppose I'll be okay—even if I am feeling miserable now.*

So, to finish off, let me give you some sisterly advice. Take it easy! Enjoy yourself! Write often. You know, penning this letter has rolled a huge, huge stone off my chest, and I feel so much better.

I am, and remain forever, your dear sister,
Rina

I folded the papers and carefully placed them into a white manila envelope. Then I stuck it into my briefcase and looked around the classroom. Many girls were engaged in conversation, this time about the Chanukah chagigah and whether it would top last year's. Of course, being seventh graders, we had no part in the chagigah at all, but from the way Chany and Yocheved were taking sides, it sounded as if they were heading it.

"And I say that the choir should come before the dances. People are interested mainly in the singing!"

"Are you for real? Look at the audience during that long *Maoz Tzur* song and you'll see—three-quarters of them are shmoozing."

"Yeah, and by the dances they're so busy looking at the dancer's feet they don't even notice the other motions!"

I turned away in exasperation. This was certainly not my idea of interesting conversation! The rest of the girls were clustered around Yael's desk, oohing and aahing over the pictures of her first nephew, born two weeks ago.

"He's adorable Yael!"

"Looks just like you—especially his eyes."

"Look at the way he crinkles his nose when he squints! Who taught him to do that?"

Who, indeed, I thought wryly. What was the big fuss about, anyway? I had seen the pictures yesterday when she left them on her desk, and came to the conclusion that a two-week-old baby looked like an old, wrinkled man.

Since there was nothing else for me to do, I thought of taking out my notes to study for biology class. No luck. Ricky wasn't finished with them yet, and sat with her forehead hunched over the papers like a scribe over his writings. So I reached into my briefcase and drew out my letter again, rereading it for a third time.

The bell rang, signaling the end of recess. It was largely ignored, since in two minutes there would be a second bell, followed by a two minute wait for the teacher. Suddenly, the school secretary walked in, clearing her throat.

"Is Leah Berger in this class?"

"That's me," I replied, my heart almost stopping as all eyes turned in my direction.

"The principal wants to speak to you," she stated flatly, then turned on her heels and left. I stood there, wondering whether to follow her.

"Do you know the way to her office, or should I show you?" asked Dina after watching me hesitate. She was sitting just a few seats away.

"That's okay, Dina, thanks. I know where it is," I replied, hoping that nobody noticed my hands were shaking.

"Okay then, good luck," she called out after me, as I left.

As I walked down the gray tiles in the long corridor I decided that I really liked Dina. She was such a nice girl. I just hoped she wasn't trying to be friendly out of pity. After all, it was obvious that Ricky was about the only girl in the class with whom I had any contact. But no, Dina wasn't that type, I soon decided, as I rounded another corner in the hallway. She was too studious and busy with herself to worry much about others' social life. She was just trying to be helpful, that's all....

I stood at the doorway to the principal's office, my insides churning like butter. Mrs. Farber opened at the first knock, her smile widening as she assessed my nervousness.

"Do come in, Leah, and sit down. Make yourself comfortable," she added, noticing me fidgeting. She went to sit behind a wide mahogany desk with two piles of papers in front of her.

"How are things going, lately?" she asked politely. I shrugged.

"Is that a positive or negative answer?" she continued, smiling.

"Things are okay, I guess," I answered, not too
convincingly.

"Your manner belies your words, but never
mind. Do you think the lessons are difficult to keep
up with?"

"My aunt hired a tutor to help me," I explained,
and she nodded.

"I recommended Miriam Feld, and I see I made
the right choice. Some of your teachers have mentioned that you have caught up with the class, and
recently I have heard reports from one of the moth-
ers as well. Actually, not directly from her..." Her
voice trailed off.

"You mean Ricky's mother?" I asked, my voice
shaking.

"Yes. And I must say, I really am proud of you.
Ricky has never done so well before, and she con-
siders you a friend. I was so impressed by what I
heard that I mentioned it to your aunt. I'm sure
that she's proud of you."

I stayed silent. How could I explain to this well-
meaning principal the harm her words had done?

"D...do you speak with Mrs. Stein often?" I ventured to ask.

"Not really, Leah. She's a busy woman, and as
long as you're doing fine, there really is no reason

to," she added as an after thought. "I just...happened to be discussing...something with her yesterday, and I told her how proud we are of you and that we are aware that you volunteered to tutor one of your classmates. That's all I wanted to tell you. Keep up the good work, Leah!" She gave me a kindly pat on my shoulder.

"Oh, and another thing. Please ask Yocheved Mann to come to my office. I want to discuss something with her, too."

I thanked her politely, and made my way to the door, wondering why Mrs. Farber hadn't been open with me. She obviously knew about the incident with the library books, yet she hadn't seen fit to mention it. And how did she find out about the tutoring? Ricky's mother wasn't the type to call.

I walked slowly down the empty hallway, not in too much of a rush. I was sure that the biology teacher was in the midst of explaining about the rodent, and I wasn't too interested. I was surprised to see the doorway to our classroom ajar, and from the hallway I could see some girls huddled around a desk at the side of the classroom. As I approached, my heart skipped a beat. I couldn't be—but yes, it was—my desk!

My footsteps quickened, and I raced into the classroom, out of breath. The teacher wasn't in the class yet. Suddenly, the group around my desk broke up and a strange quiet descended upon the classroom. Everyone seemed embarrassed to look at the others, and they seemed to be avoiding my eyes also. Or did I imagine it?

"Yocheved, Mrs. Farber wants to see you in her office," I turned to her, trying to make my voice sound natural.

Without a word, she turned and walked out of the classroom. It looked like she was escaping.

"Hey, did my face turn green?" I asked, half jokingly, turning to Chany.

She shrugged, looking away. Since the day I told the girls the fib about my family moving here, I hadn't really shown my humorous nature. Squaring my jaw, I turned and walked to my desk.

And then I saw it. The letter. It lay open and exposed on my desk, forlorn and creased. It must have been read. I felt raw and hollow, like I was made of glass and the girls—how many of them had there been?—now they had seen straight through me.

I didn't even notice Ricky sidling up until she was right beside me. "They read your letter. I wanted to say something, but I didn't realize what was happening until it was too late!"

The classroom swam before my eyes. Grabbing the letter, I stuffed it into my briefcase. Then I snatched my briefcase, turned and ran, almost colliding into the biology teacher at the door.

"Where do you think you're going, Leah?" she asked me. I edged past her, ignoring the question.

For I didn't know the answer myself. All I wanted to do was disappear—from my classmates whom I couldn't face, now that they knew the truth about me. I raced down the corridors blindly and out the main doorway to the school yard, my mind a blank. It was only once I was safely on the street that I realized where I wanted to go.

Runaway

ighteen Elm Drive. I found it without too much trouble, after a half hour of wandering. Remember, I had been living with the Steins for a while, and had some chance to become familiar with the winding streets. It turned out that Elm Drive was just a few short blocks from Elm Place.

Hesitantly, I walked up the graveled front path, lifted the brass knocker and knocked twice. How familiar and homey the house appeared! Its grimy windows looked warm and friendly, the untrimmed shrubs so welcoming. Slowly, I relaxed from my frenzied flight, and excited about my new plan I waited for the door to open.

I stood by the door waiting for what seemed like

an eternity, and so I lifted the knocker again. Before I could drop it, I heard muffled footsteps. Then the door was slowly opened, and I stood facing Mrs. Kassel. She had the same bewildered expression on her sweet face from when I had last seen her almost two months before.

"Who is it?" she asked, peering at me closely. Her hair still seemed astonishingly white and her cat's eye glasses were perched on the same wrinkled face.

"It's me—the girl you thought was your *einikel* Kreindel, remember?"

"Oy, my Kreindel!" she reached out to embrace me, then quickly stepped back. "But you aren't Kreindel, are you?"

"No, Mrs. Kassel, I am not Kreindel. You made the same mistake last time too. Don't you remember?"

"Ah, you are the sweet little girl who came to my house... I remember now! Come in, come in darling!" She ushered me in with such delight that my heart warmed over.

"So tell me, how are things going with you? I'm so glad you came for a visit." She spoke to me while I sprawled, exhausted, on the musty couch in the living room.

"Well, I came here because I finally made up my mind. Remember when you asked me if I want to stay here? I have the answer now. I really would like to live with you. I can help you cook and clean, and will be like another granddaughter."

Instead of clapping her hands in joy like I expected, her face took on a look of consternation.

"Oy, vay! What a pity! I wish you could stay with me darling, but I am moving to a senior citizen's center in a few months. It is too lonely for me here, and my daughter, she's selling the house."

"Selling the house? Oh no! Why are you going to do that?" I was horrified at the prospect of this spunky woman losing her independence. I couldn't imagine her living with lots of old ladies.

"Well," she seemed to hesitate, "With my rheumatism and stiff back, it is hard for me to bend. I am all alone, and have no one to help me. So maybe it will be a good idea for me to live with other people like me. All of us will help each other."

"When did you decide to move?" I asked.

"Last week my daughter, Pessel, and my son, Haskel, came to visit, and they talked and talked and talked until...." she spread her hands open in a gesture of defeat. "Two days ago they sold the house—they got a lot of money—and next Sunday they will take me to see the center for myself. A comfortable building, they say. But why do you look so disappointed, darling? A beautiful girl like you!"

How could I describe to this lonely, gentle lady how I felt?

My last hope, my only recourse was shattered. I

had thought I could ask Uncle Michael if I could stay at this old woman's house, until he could find me another home. For I was sure of one thing. I could no longer return to the Steins and their "classy" school. I had had enough of that life, and it was time for a change.

With Mrs. Kassel's permission, I dialed Uncle Michael's number at work, hoping he would be there and answer. No such luck. His assistant said he wasn't in. I tried Aunt Shifra at home, but the phone was busy.

"So, tell me darling. Where have you been living until now? What happened to make you come and want to live with me? Tell me the whole story. I promise I won't make you more upset."

With infinite patience I sat and explained my circumstances to Mrs. Kassel, until her head bobbed up and down in sympathy. She reached for a tissue to dry the tears that were welling out of the corners of her eyes. I guess I *was* a little too dramatic!

"Don't worry, darling. At my age one cries for every little thing. I understand how you are feeling, but don't worry—as I always tell my Kreindel when she is sad—things will get better."

I wandered around the untidy house following Mrs. Kassel as she went about her chores. I wondered whether the school had alerted the Steins and if they were looking for me. Not that I really cared. It was just—well, a curious feeling to wonder if I was an object of worry. In truth, I kind of wanted to know whether somebody cared enough to find out where I was.

A while later, I finally reached Uncle Michael at work. As soon as I heard his voice I burst into tears. Sobbing, I related the whole story while Mrs. Kassel stood by solicitously with tissues.

"So you ran off from school and went straight there, I imagine," he paused.

"Uncle Michael, did I have any choice? I couldn't face the girls, knowing that they had read my private letter and knew all about—my difficulties—I don't think anyone could have stayed in that classroom knowing that—"

"But Leah," my uncle's maddeningly, reasonable voice interrupted, "Are you really sure they read the letter?"

"Ricky told me," I hotly retorted. "I trust Ricky!!"

"Ricky who?"

"That's my new friend, the girl I tutor, that made Mrs. Stein so angry at me to begin with."

"Leah, do you want me to call the Steins for you?"

"No, well okay, I guess," I conceded, defeated. I could tell Uncle Michael didn't really want me back, or he would have offered. As desperate as I was, I was too proud to ask. I left him my number, and put down the phone, feeling deflated and out of place in the great, wide world. I couldn't think of a place in the entire universe where I was wanted.

I wondered if any of my carefree classmates could ever understand how it felt not to have a home where you really belonged. And I guessed I would never again know what it felt like to live with my own father and mother who really loved me, with a sister to fight and play with. As I stood in Mrs. Kassel's kitchen, I silently vowed to try, to the best of my ability, (with Hashem's help, of course,) to give my own children that which I had been denied.

After drying my tears and eating a few peaches from Mrs. Kassel's fridge, I wandered about her living room, looking at pictures and keeping her company. At length the phone rang again, and I rushed to answer it.

"Hello?"

"Hello? Is that you, Rina?"

"Susan!?" My voice rose in delight, but she quickly interrupted.

"Where have you been? I've been so nervous worrying about you. Believe it or not, so is Jenny. She's usually so calm when everyone else is going crazy."

"And...Mrs. Stein?" I asked, scarcely daring to breathe. I couldn't believe that I actually cared enough to ask that question.

"Your aunt is hysterical. The principal called and said you were missing, and she's not been herself since then. She sent Butch to search for you—we couldn't imagine where you went. Your uncle even came home from work. We almost called the police. *Boruch Hashem*, your Uncle Michael called and told us where you were!" Susan recounted all this so quickly I could barely understand her. "Butch is on his way to pick you up."

"But Susan, I'm not coming back home," I said, with a force that surprised me. Strange, how the word "home" slipped out of my tongue. Was it really my home?

"Call Butch on the car phone and tell him to make a u-turn! I refuse to live in a house where I am not wanted, and you can tell Mrs. Stein I said that!" I felt really determined now.

"There's no time for explanations now. You just come on home and you'll see that things will be different. I think running away was the best thing you could have done. You got them all shaken up and there was a lot of talking about how much they want you back. So come and see for yourself."

I was surprised that what I had done had "shaken them up."

"Do you really mean it, Susan?" I asked suspiciously, not knowing whether to trust her words. I knew that she wanted me to come back, but what about the others?

Honk! Honk! The familiar honk of the black Lincoln Town Car interrupted our conversation. "I hear someone honking and if it's Butch you had better not keep him waiting!" Susan warned, her voice lower and more serious. I said goodbye and hung up.

"I have to go now!" I called out to Mrs. Kassel, though there were misgivings in my heart. In any case, I knew I couldn't stay with her much longer, and I guess there was nowhere else I could go.

"Goodbye and thank you so much for everything! You've been so nice to me."

"Goodbye, darling! Don't forget me! Come visit me at the senior citizen's center. Here's my new address and phone number," she said, handing me the center's business card. "Don't forget about me, darling!" she repeated.

I gave her a heartfelt hug and walked out the door and into the car, feeling as if I were being taken to the guillotine. I was nervous and frightened. How would the Steins greet me after my disappearance? Would they be mad? Yell? Punish me?

"I do have a choice," I told myself. "I can tell Butch to stop the car, and I can jump out. Then I could go to...where?" I suddenly realized, with sinking horror, that I was truly homeless. I had no place to call home!

The short ride passed too quickly and soon I was back in the front foyer, which was eerily silent. As I tiptoed behind Butch, my mind was a whirlwind of conflicting thoughts. Why did I let myself be talked into coming back here? This wasn't really where I belonged!

Squaring my jaw, I stepped into the brightly lit kitchen, and stopped in my tracks. I could see Mr. Stein sitting in the adjacent study, hunched over a newspaper. I could see his shoulders tense as he heard my footsteps, but he didn't look up. His wife was standing in the corner of the kitchen, conferring with Jenny in hushed tones.

Susan was nowhere to be seen.

I cleared my throat, and took another step which brought me near the kitchen table. Jenny turned toward me, relief written all over her rosy face. I was even surprised to find that her eyes were red as if she had been crying.

"Leah, so you're here! You must have had a hard day! Come, I'll help you wash up and I'm sure you're starving. Susan has prepared cheese blintzes especially for you."

I merely stared at her. Jenny had never spoken so solicitously to me. Was this some sort of trick?

"I...uh...don't know if I'm hungry, Jenny. I'd rather go up to my room."

Mrs. Stein came forward, her face haggard and pale. She too looked like she had been crying.

"Welcome home, Leah! I was so worried about you!" And then, without warning, she came over to me and gave me a hug. I shrank back, ignoring the hurt look in her eyes.

"Leah, please go upstairs, wash up and change,

then come back down here. We've got a lot to discuss, and you probably want to rest after your hectic day...."

Mutely, like an obedient robot, I went upstairs, washed and changed into a robe. Then I came down and dully took my place at the table. Jenny had gone to her duties and Mr. and Mrs. Stein were waiting for me.

"So you picked yourself up and ran off, eh?" Mr. Stein began. "You gave the school administration quite a scare. They called here to see if you were home. When there was no answer, they alerted us at work. We couldn't imagine where you had run off to, but they assured us that you couldn't be too far. I give the school a lot of credit, that I do. Very organized place, I must say. I'm impressed with that principal. She's a real *mentch*. It takes a very responsible person to deal with an organization as large as your school."

Mr. Stein had a tendency to drone on and on about a subject, but his wife gave him a look which meant, "get down to business already."

"Okay, okay. Let me get to the point immediately," he cleared his throat and then looked up at me with a concerned look on his face. "Why did you run away, Leah?"

I was a little taken back by his directness. In answer to the sincerity in his eyes and his honest, candid manner, my eyes filled with tears. He reached for a handkerchief from his pocket and handed it to me.

"Please don't cry, Leah. Tell us what upset you. We really would like to correct it. You know, we want you to be happy."

I could hardly think coherently I was so unprepared for his genuine concern and directness. But I managed to organize my thoughts just a little bit.

"From the way you've been treating me here, it sure doesn't seem like you care if I am happy or not," I said a little too sullenly, looking in Aunt Beth's direction. "You don't even grant me the basic right to lead my own life and decide my own friendships. You've invaded my room at all hours and confiscated my personal property. You've twisted around praise from the principal and turned it into an insult. And then you say you want me to be happy?!"

There was a silent pause.

"Leah, what you are saying is all news to me," Mr. Stein declared. "I know nothing of all these happenings. It's partly my fault. I've been extremely busy with my business, and I come home too exhausted to pay much attention to this big, rambling house.

"Unfortunately I do not see to the day-to-day affairs of this house. Beth takes care of any problems when they arise. I see that I've been wrong. I should have taken more of an interest in you to begin with."

I stared at Uncle Gerald, and comprehension set in. Could it be that it had been his idea to bring me here all along? Was he the one who was related to me? Was Aunt Beth merely my aunt by marriage? But that didn't make sense. Aunt Shifra had told me that Aunt Beth was once very close to their—to our family.

"Did you know that Leah was so unhappy?" Mr. Stein asked his wife.

"Leah was doing fine until she decided to spend all night reading novels, neglecting her schoolwork, risking her health, not getting enough sleep and spending two afternoons a week with a learning-disabled classmate," Aunt Beth said carefully, trying not to look at me. What she said was true, and yet...how wrong was her assessment! I had not been fine until then. I had been—I was still—dying for a friend, for something with which to fill my empty hours. There was so much I could say in my defense! Instead I stubbornly said nothing.

Luckily, I didn't need to. Uncle Gerald came to my defense.

"But, Beth, from the way the situation appears, the principal seems to be quite satisfied with Rina's progress. Why don't we let her continue with her projects?"

"I don't want her to fall behind in her studies. She is so brilliant and gifted. She should not have to settle for anything less than the best. The principal said she was doing okay, but not spectacularly. I think she's losing a big opportunity to excel by reading novels and tutoring others!" said Mrs. Stein, her voice quavering with emotion.

"Why have you chosen only one girl as your friend?" she continued, turning to me, genuine puzzlement in her face. Her voice sounded hurt as she asked, "Can't you make friends with some of the other girls? I hired a tutor especially so that you could get good marks and do well, leaving you with time to cultivate real friendships."

"Ricky is a real friend!" I snapped. Although I knew that wasn't quite true. "And besides, why do you care about my choice of friends? You make it sound like I'm worthless unless everyone admires me! Don't you like me as I am?" I blurted out.

"Of course I do, Leah, of course I do," she reiterated, her voice sounding strangely vulnerable. "I thought you knew that. I know that sometimes I'm very strict and unyielding but I really don't mean to be. I just want the best for you."

Before I was able to fully digest what she was saying, my cold, rigid aunt burst into tears. I stared at her, shocked.

"I think we all need to clear the air," said Mr. Stein softly. "Leah, by now it should be clear to you that we care about you. We invited you to our home because we wanted you to join our family. We think you're a sweet, special girl and it's been a joy having you here. Is that clear?" He paused and looked at me with tenderness.

I nodded, not trusting my voice. I don't consider myself a cry baby, but this conversation was a little more than I had bargained for. I tried to control my tears but, if Mrs. Stein was crying, somehow I didn't feel foolish to do the same.

When we both had calmed down somewhat, Uncle Gerald gently asked me what had happened in school that day.

I just told them everything—there was nothing to lose—I began from the first day of school when I had felt like an outsider, going on to my relationship with Ricky and the chain of events that led to my running away. Though my voice faltered at times, I didn't leave out a single detail. The Steins listened intently, not saying a word.

"I see," said Uncle Gerald, after a long pause.

"Strange, the principal didn't say anything about a letter. She merely mentioned that the girls said you had sounded upset, grabbed your briefcase, and ran away from school."

"Mrs. Farber doesn't know everything," I retorted. "How can she? Do you expect Yocheved and Chany to come up to her and say, 'Hey, we read the letter Leah wrote to her sister, and now we all know she's a pathetic orphan?' Or maybe they should announce in the hallway that I have no mother and my only relatives are miles away? That I'm a liar and I make up stories about myself?"

When I finished, Mrs. Stein had turned red. Mr. Stein looked away. Nobody spoke for a while. When my uncle did speak, he sounded evasive.

"Leah, you don't have to go back to school yet. You deserve a few days off. I'm sure the tutor will help you catch up quickly," he continued, seeing that his wife did not agree with the plan.

"Who says I'm going back to school?" I challenged. "For that matter, who says I'm staying here at all?"

As soon as the words were out, I could have bitten my tongue. But it was too late.

"Do you want to go back to your Aunt Shifra and Uncle Michael?" Aunt Beth asked carefully.

"Do I? Of course I do. But they don't want me. Nobody wants me. I'm just an unwanted girl with no real home, no family and no place to go. And I can't even see my sister, the only person who really loves me!"

"Leah, how can you say that?" asked Uncle Gerald, looking a little aghast at my melodrama. "Didn't we just finish telling you that we really wanted you, Leah Berger, not your brains, or your marks, or anything else?"

"Y...yes," I hiccuped. "I know it here," I pointed to my head. "But I don't feel it here," I said placing my hand on my heart.

"That will come with time, Leah," said my uncle. Aunt Beth was still too distraught to speak, dabbing at her eyes with a tissue. She probably felt ridiculous crying in front of me.

"I think you are simply homesick, and miss your sister very much. I have an idea. I can't believe we didn't think of it earlier! What would you say if we arranged for your sister to come visit you during Chanukah vacation?"

I stared at him, open-mouthed, not believing what I heard.

"D...do you really mean it?" I said.

"I sure do," he replied sounding like he really meant it and grinning at me. "I think it'll do both of you a world of good."

"Yippee!" I said, jumping up and down, feeling like my former self again. Aunt Beth and Uncle Gerald looked at each other and smiled, I guess relieved that they finally figured out something that would make me happy.

"So it's settled then. You'll stay with us, I hope?" he asked.

I nodded carefully. Of course I would stay with them! What other choice did I have? But there was one thing that I wanted to make clear. "But I don't want to go back to Bais Yaakov ever again. I can't face those girls!"

"Not going back to school, I'm afraid, is not a solution," he replied. "It may be uncomfortable for you the first few days, but as time goes by, you'll be glad the girls finally know the truth. Of course—" he continued, seeing that I was about to protest, "I can understand how you would rather it wouldn't have come out like that, but now that it did, you'll make the best of it. Maybe it was *bashert*, and will be the start of many new friendships. And maybe it's better that everyone now knows so you don't have to tell everyone."

"I don't need to be friends with those snobs. I have Ricky, and there's another nice girl, her name is Dina..." my voice trailed off as Aunt Beth looked at me questioningly.

"I'm sure that this Ricky you have mentioned is as sweet and fine as the others, if not more. I'm glad that you've been helping her out," Mr. Stein carefully replied, sounding like a therapist. "However, it's possible that by focusing just on her, you've been sending a subtle message to the rest of the girls in your class to keep away. This may be in part why you're feeling so unhappy, why you read in your room until 2:00 a.m."

"I don't read in my room anymore," I said, feeling deflated remembering the humiliating library experience. "I have no more books."

"Ahem..." Aunt Beth cleared her throat. "I have...er...reconsidered. The librarian called me yesterday and we had a long talk. I have decided to allow you the privilege of reading one book a week, strictly before your bedtime, of course, and once your homework is done."

"Thank you, Aunt Beth," I said, my eyes shining with gratitude.

"You're most welcome," she said softly, "my dear Leah."

I made my way up to my room slowly, my mind a kaleidoscope of decisions and thoughts. Fragments of the conversation floated around me. That night, I slept like a baby. For the first time since I had arrived at my new home, I felt at peace.

I remembered the conversation I had had with Malky, when I had told her to think positively. Now I was the one who needed to learn how to count my blessings and be grateful for whatever I had. I knew it wouldn't be easy.

So much had happened during the past week! Just when I had begun to adjust to my new home, the library book incident came along to make me feel like an intruder in the Stein's home. And then my running away...and discovering, to my surprise, how much the Stein's missed me when I came back. It was comforting to realize that the Steins truly wanted to give me a home because they cared about me, and *not* because they pitied me. Yet something about the Steins felt spooky and mysterious. It was as if they were hiding something. There was so much I didn't know. I still never did find out why Aunt Shifra didn't like the Steins.

Would I ever find out?

The next day, I noticed an immediate difference in the atmosphere. At the breakfast table it was like the calm after the storm. My aunt's smile was softer, more genuine, less forced. She seemed to carefully consider her words before she spoke. My uncle's expression radiated encouragement, Susan was effusive and loving, and even Jenny's frigid manner had warmed up. In contrast, it was cold outside; the first snowstorm of the season had frozen the trees into grotesque shapes. Bare branches sported jagged icicles.

After the Steins went to work I was left alone with my thoughts. I stood at the glass patio door, drinking it all in. There was something about the crispness of winter that bespoke freshness and change.

On an impulse, I opened the door a crack and stuck my head out; the frosty air sucked my breath away, and the wind whispered promises of renewal. Chanukah was three weeks away. I looked at my watch. It was 11 a.m.—there was a five hour time difference between London and New York. At 1 p.m. I would call Malky—she got home from school 6 p.m. London time. I couldn't wait to tell her the good news. I waited impatiently for the hours to pass. Finally it was time.

"Hello?"

"Malky?"

"Rina?"

"Malky? Guess what?" my words tumbled over each other in excitement.

"What?"

"You're coming!"

"I'm what?"

"You're coming to visit me! That is, if Aunt Rachel agrees."

"Wow! I can't believe it. Oh, I hope she says okay!"

"If she agrees, the Steins will send you a ticket to come on Chanukah vacation," I said, breathing into the phone.

There was a long pause. "Oh, Rina," Malky finally said. "I'm so excited I can't speak!"

"Then we'll wait until we meet in person. Three more weeks."

"Three more weeks," Malky replied.

We both were counting the days.

I spent the rest of the day klutzing and enjoying myself immensely, thrilled at the day off from school. I was grateful the Steins had given me time to adjust to the new reality, to grapple with everything that had happened.

Evening came early, the stars twinkling in the frosty sky. After supper, I received a phone call. To my delight, it was from Ricky. After chatting happily for a few seconds, tactfully avoiding the subject of my disappearance and the reaction it caused, I tried to figure out why Ricky called.

"Do you and Bina miss studying with me? Maybe my aunt will give me permission and I can come again starting tomorrow."

"Uh, don't worry about that so much, Rina. Believe it or not, since we've stopped the lessons, I've been continuing to study by myself—every night! As soon as the house is quiet and the kids are in bed I go into my private cubbyhole—the large walk-in closet in the children's room, and study my head off! I even got a 90% on yesterday's halacha test!"

"That's fantastic! Did Mrs. Mandel write a comment?"

"No, but she looked at me in a funny sort of way, as if she wasn't sure it was really me! And, you know what, when she handed that paper back to me I was positive it wasn't mine!!"

"Ricky, you were capable of that 90% all along!" I declared. "All you needed was a little push."

"I know. That's what the principal mentioned at yesterday's class discussion."

"What discussion?"

"Didn't you get any other phone calls today?"

"Don't tease me, Ricky. You know you're the only friend I've got, no competition!"

"Well, you won't believe what I'm telling you, but I promise it's true. After lunch yesterday, Mrs. Farber came into our class and spoke to all of us—about you. She went on and on about what a special girl you are, coming from the Midwest and accomplishing so much in such a short amount of time. She spoke about you tutoring one of our sisters—and every head turned in my direction.

"I thought I would die of shame—except that the principal didn't notice and continued talking like nothing had happened. Then a lot of the girls asked for your phone number and she gave it and told them to be more friendly and welcoming to you and—

Why, Rina—are you listening? You haven't said a word!"

I stood frozen near the phone, ear on the receiver, not believing what I had heard.

"Ricky...," I finally stammered. "Please repeat everything you just said—in the correct order."

Half an hour later, I had the story straight. Apparently, Mr. Stein had done his job well. After the principal was apprised of my situation, she "decided" to set things straight by encouraging the other girls in my class to "aspire" to "win my hand" in friendship. Yuck! Some people just have no tact, and the worst part of it is when they think they do.

"Whew! That was a tough one! Thanks for letting me know of it, Ricky. You're a true pal."

"No problem. I'm sure you would have done the same for me. I knew you would like to hear what's been going on."

"No kidding! And I'm give it to any girl who dares

come over to me with a phony smile to ask how I've been feeling these past few days. At least they'll see that I'm not a chesed case, waiting for some T.L.C.!"

"Don't take it to heart, Rina. If I wanted to, I could be even more embarrassed than you are. After all, now everybody knows why we're always going to my house to 'study'. Doesn't do much good for my name, does it?"

"Don't be silly, Ricky," I said attempting to placate her. "The fact that you have a learning-disabled sister is no reflection on you. What you make of yourself is what counts!"

"Listen to yourself talking, Rina. You sound just like the principal!"

"Why, that's the last person I want to sound like!"

"But you do. Because when she spoke to us yesterday, she stressed the idea that nobody chooses their set of circumstances in life, that the main thing is to make the most of what you are given, and that *you*, Rina, are the best example of that!"

"Is that what she really thinks?" I asked suspiciously.

"You had better believe it. After she left everyone was extremely quiet, and then Yocheved spoke up, saying how bad she feels for being so nasty to you— about what a special girl you are—doing so much chesed in your own quiet way. Then Chany piped up and said that you are a genius—that to the best of her knowledge you always get 100% on every test. And they decided to write an apology note to you for reading your letter."

"Wha—how did they know I knew about the letter?!" I asked, surprised.

"How did they know? As soon as you walked into the classroom you had that stunned look on your face. You snatched up your papers and stalked right out—bumping into the biology teacher—and since you didn't return to school today, how can you still wonder how they knew?"

"Okay, okay, perhaps you have a point. Still, I don't need their friendship, as much as it's worth."

"Okay, Gotta go now," said Ricky, after an awkward pause. I glanced at my watch. We had been on the phone for almost an hour!

"Bye Ricky. You know what—you're a true friend!" I said.

"Likewise," Ricky replied, and hung up the phone.

I massaged my sore neck, which had been balancing the receiver, and went upstairs to review my schoolwork. A new school day was waiting for me tomorrow.

That night, I had trouble falling asleep. I was too excited, too nervous, too high-strung with worries and expectations. Would my classmates accept me? Would they treat me differently than they had before they knew my story?

Finally, at 12:30 a.m., I grew tired of tossing and turning. I threw off my covers, and got out of bed, groping for my slippers. Then I made my way down the stairs to get a drink of milk. I had heard that warm milk makes you sleepy.

Halfway down the landing, I saw a light and heard voices coming from the kitchen. At first I was frightened, but then I recognized the Steins' voices. I stopped, and strained to pay attention.

"Doing great work in school...a real asset to her class," said Aunt Beth.

"I told you you'd be proud of her," replied Uncle Gerald.

"When she ran away, it hurt so much...it was like losing Devorah all over again," whispered Aunt Beth her voice cracking.

"Shh...don't think about it," said her husband in a soothing voice. "Drink your tea. It's very late."

As I heard her chair scrape back, I pattered up the stairs, bewildered and frightened. Who was Devorah and when did Aunt Beth lose her?

It seems there were lots of mysteries I knew nothing about. I ran back into my bed trying to figure out who this Devorah could be. Finally, I fell into a confused, dreamless sleep.

A New Beginning

"I'll drive Leah to school today," Mr. Stein generously offered, the next morning, a Wednesday. Butch had called in sick, and I surprised the Steins by appearing right on time dressed in the gray plaid skirt and matching vest that meant school, my briefcase in hand.

"No, you don't really have to, Uncle Gerald. I'm sure you're very busy. I'll take the school bus," I feebly protested.

"Butch won't be in today, which is why I'm taking the car, although the parking will be impractical," Uncle Gerald explained. When he saw that I still didn't agree, he tried to persuade me.

"It's my pleasure, Leah. Really it is. I have an

important document to bring to my office, so we have to stop there for a few minutes. We'll leave as soon as you've eaten. You'll take the other car, Beth, unless you want to come right now?"

"No, later will be just fine, thank you. I have to stay and give the plumber instructions about fixing the sink. He's been so negligent lately, and I haven't been on top of the situation. I'll call you as soon as I'm done."

I had the feeling they were doing this on purpose—that Mr. Stein wanted to talk to me alone, but I didn't have too much time to think about it. I ate quickly, trying not to stuff the french toast into my mouth, and *bentched.* Then I bolted from my seat and joined Mr. Stein, who was waiting at the door.

"My that was a quick breakfast!" Susan commented. "Enjoy yourself at school and come home in a good mood." I threw her a kiss on my way out. Jenny, standing at the door, looked the other way. Did it bother her that I had such a good relationship with Susan? I wondered. Maybe there was more to her than her tough exterior let on.

We rode in companionable silence for a time, unbroken except for the rhythmic humming of the motor. Mr. Stein looked lost in deep thought, and I stared out the window at the stately houses lined up at the side of the road. They looked like they were competing with each other for attention.

"So are you ready for school, Leah?" my uncle

asked, his voice softening. I looked up, startled out of my reverie, and tried to think of an answer.

"Well, yes and no. I'm still trying to figure out how to face the girls and their phony smiles."

"There's only one way to react to a phony smile," he said, in all seriousness.

"Huh?" I asked, curious.

"Smile back. And don't let on that you know it's a fake. If they see your smile is for real, their smiles will also be sincere. That's human nature, and it never fails to work. And remember, any time you need a pep talk, I'm here to help."

The stop at his office took longer than expected, and I twiddled my fingers in the back seat of the car, while the second-hand on my watch ticked irritatingly. When he finally rushed towards the car, looking very apologetic, it was already five to nine, and I knew that I would have to make a grand entrance into class.

"Sorry, Leah. My secretary wasn't sure about our new computer system. You know how these things are."

"Don't worry about it," I assured him, fibbing. "We're not that late yet."

We drove up to the school and I stepped out, wondering if my nonchalant expression hid my turbulent emotions. I walked down the familiar hallways, hoping I wouldn't meet anyone in the halls. Not that I was likely to, for the bell had rung more than seven minutes earlier. The halls buzzed with the sound of discussion and teachers lecturing.

Entering my classroom was easier than I had expected. Mrs. Mandel was animatedly explaining a difficult passage, and I handed her my late note, slipping into my seat beside Ricky, ignoring all the stares. Ricky flashed me an ear-to-ear smile, and showed me the place in my halacha notebook.

Suddenly, when the lesson was almost over, we heard static over the intercom, and the secretary's voice came through the wires. "Attention, students: grades seven through twelve are to immediately report to the auditorium for an assembly." As the intercom switched off, the teacher closed her notebook and the room became a beehive of activity.

"Hey, pssst. What do you think it's all about?" Yocheved turned to Yael.

"How should I know?" Yael shrugged, and then I saw—or thought I saw—Chany winking significantly at them. The threesome huddled together, and for a split second, I felt like joining them. The desire to belong quickly disappeared, to be replaced with, "who needs them?"

The large auditorium became noisy as all the girls entered, talking animatedly. Soon, the students were sitting in neat rows, waiting with barely suppressed excitement as the principal got up on stage. Mrs. Farber waited until the noise died down, and began in her best stage-voice.

"You probably are all wondering what this sudden assembly is all about. Well, I won't keep you in suspense for too long. But first, let me begin with a story that is familiar to us all.

There was once a proud father who had ten strong sons, all loyal and obedient to him. When he felt his end was near, he asked them to gather around his bed. To their surprise, he held a bundle of twigs, passing it around to all the sons, and asked them to break it in half. One by one, they tried and strained, but the twigs refused to budge. 'Hand them back to me now,' he commanded. With a smile, the father untied the bundle, and passed around the ten twigs, one to each son. Now they broke with a snap.

'The message is clear,' the father said, looking at each of his sons in turn. 'When you are all united, no power on earth can break you. Let discord and contention prevail, and you will be weak men.'"

Mrs. Farber paused, looking around the auditorium; the room felt thick with emotion.

"What does this story teach us, girls?" she asked. Everyone looked at her expectantly.

"*Achdus*! When we, as a school are united, with friendship and understanding, no power on earth can break us. Take the word "united" and move around two letters. What do you get? Untied! With one subtle comment or put down, we can untie the special spirit this school has worked so hard to achieve. It is in our hands to make it or break it."

As the principal paused to take a break, the exuberant eleventh graders broke into a rousing *achdus* song, and the entire auditorium soon was clapping along.

After around ten minutes of singing Mrs. Farber continued.

"That's the spirit, girls. Now, you probably are wondering what made me decide to call an *achdus* assembly in the middle of the year.

"As you all know, the elementary Bais Yaakov, our parent school, has been trying to implement a tutoring program for some of their students. The classes there keep growing, *bli ayin hora*, and some of the girls cannot keep up. The elementary principal has asked me to organize a group of junior high and high school girls to work together with the weaker students, perhaps on a weekly basis. I was hesitant at first, knowing how busy all of you are with your own schoolwork. But just this week one of our seventh graders proved that it's possible to not only take care of others but to keep up with your own responsibilities."

She took a deep breath and looked (or did it only seem like it?) straight at me. I quickly glanced down, feeling more eyes upon me—those of my admiring classmates.

The rest of the assembly passed in a blur. The principal explained the details of the program, and the girls were all for it. Even the juniors and high-and-mighty seniors were heatedly discussing the idea as we flocked to our classrooms. My face was flushed, and I felt uncomfortable, yet proud. All because of my idea! But the best was yet to come, the icing on the cake....

"Leah...I uh...we want to apologize for reading the letter," Yocheved and Chany stood together, looking uncomfortable, their faces suddenly reddening. "We had no idea...it was...I mean...we're sorry."

I took a deep breath, and said one word: "Forgiven."

Just like that I forgave them—them and the rest of the class. Maybe I was just so desperate to become popular. I don't know.

At English recess, Mrs. Farber stopped by our classroom to discuss the tutoring program. Each student was to go home and ask her parents for permission to devote an hour a week to help a Bais Yaakov girl with homework. Although she would only need five girls from our class, and not every girl in the class would be a suitable tutor, it was good to have a few extras lined up, just in case.

"And another thing," the principal added. "Those of you who will be tutoring may not use it as an excuse to fall behind in any aspect of your own studies."

♦ ♦ ♦

"So how did it go today, Rina?" Susan patted me

affectionately on the back when I returned that day. I was absolutely exhausted yet on top of the world.

"Oh, amazingly great!" I gushed. "Our principal organized a terrific assembly, where she introduced a tutoring program, and girls from all the grades will help younger girls with their homework. And it was all my idea!"

Susan nodded understandingly, the smile on her face spreading to the wrinkles beneath her eyes.

"And how did it go about the letter?" she asked cautiously, looking over her shoulder. Jenny was not in the kitchen area, luckily for me. I don't know why, but I found it hard to confide in Susan when Jenny was around. Jenny wasn't nasty or mean, she was just so cold and proper, that I didn't feel comfortable sharing my thoughts with her.

But Susan was waiting for an answer. "Oh, the letter? I almost forgot about it already," I replied. "The girls apologized and that was that. I mean, it was pretty embarrassing, and they had some nerve, but I'm sort of happier and relieved that they know now, and I don't have to keep on hiding."

My voice trailed off as my teeth sank into a fragrant fresh-out-of-the-oven cinnamon bun. Then I dug into my briefcase, pulled out the infamous letter to Malky, ripped it into shreds and threw it into the garbage.

Later, when Mr. Stein came home, I approached

him with a request. "Can I have a nice piece of stationary, please? I want to write my sister a letter. Of course, she'll probably arrive here before the letter gets there—airmail is so slow—but I'm feeling so great right now, I want to tell Malky about everything that has happened."

I noticed my uncle beaming from ear to ear, thrilled that his plan had worked. But thankfully he didn't say anything about it and just replied to my question.

"My pleasure. Come with me into the study."

I followed him eagerly. His study was officially off limits, and I had never been there with permission before. The room smelled of rich, dark wood; floor to ceiling bookcases lined all three walls, and there was a handsome, oak desk in the center. A large plush, leather office chair and a recliner completed the scene.

Uncle Gerald rummaged in his desk until he found what he wanted—an elaborate, beige writing pad with a monogrammed "S" for Stein. It was an elegant piece of stationary, but the initial wasn't mine.

"But uncle, "I said hesitantly. "My last name begins with a 'B', not an 'S'!"

"Use it now, and we'll order you another writing pad, with your initial."

"Oh, thank you so much!"

There were more surprises in store for me. "Leah,

Beth has a surprise for you, but she'll be working late today. She wanted to take you out shopping, to get you a new dress for our anniversary party."

"Anniversary party?" I hadn't heard any talk about that before.

"Yes. Next Tuesday is our twenty-ninth wedding anniversary, *b'ezras Hashem.* I understand Susan is planning a special supper, sort of a little party. Beth wanted to invite a few of our friends to help us celebrate, but I convinced her that it would be nice to eat a dinner together, just the three of us," he winked at me.

"Um...uh...I wanted to ask...," I began, not sure of what to say next.

"Yes, Leah? Is anything the matter?"

"N...no. I just thought that maybe...if Aunt Beth is busy...maybe I can shop for a dress myself? With a friend, of course," I hastened to assure him.

"Hmm...that doesn't sound like a bad idea. I'm not sure how Beth will react, but I think you're old enough. Besides, we're so busy at the office these days..."

"Then I can go?" I asked hopefully.

"Yes, you can. I'll work on your aunt, and try to get her to agree. How about tomorrow?"

"Tomorrow sounds great," I said, excited. My first shopping trip, alone. This was going to be fun! "Maybe I can take a friend along," I suggested. My uncle nodded. "Later," he said, turning to the pile of papers on his desk. I waited on pins and needles for suppertime, when I was sure the conversation would come up.

As I had thought, it was every bit as much fun as I had expected. Aunt Beth didn't love the idea, but Uncle Gerald insisted.

"There's a Saks Fifth Avenue not too far from here at the big shopping center in Garden City. They are open late tomorrow night," my uncle said, taking two hundred dollar bills out of his wallet and placing them in an envelope. "Be careful with this money; hold on to your pocketbook tightly!"

"Ask the saleslady to show you the most elegant line," Aunt Beth repeated, for the fifth time. "And don't worry about the money. Now are you sure your friend Ricky knows where to go?"

"She's been there so many times," I fibbed, irritated at her overbearing "mother hen" attitude. (Oh, sure, Ricky went shopping in the fancy department stores in Garden City! I'm sure she got most of her clothes from hand-me-downs just like I used to when my mother was still alive. I wondered if she would accept an outfit if I bought it for her, and if my aunt would agree. But not this time. I didn't want to start another disagreement, especially now, when they were being so nice to me.

"I'm sure you won't get lost," my aunt replied. "It's just that...well...I feel responsible for you, and I'm frightened to let you go somewhere alone. What if..." Her voice trailed off, and I noticed she had suddenly become quite pale.

"Are you all right, Beth?" Uncle Gerald asked solicitously.

"I'm fine," she said, though apparently she was not. "I think I'll go upstairs." She excused herself from the table, and left. A strained silence descended over the dinette. What was this all about? All I wanted was to go shopping alone. I wasn't asking to go to Mars! What was the matter with her? I was sure most of my classmates didn't have to go through all this in order to receive permission for a shopping trip. On the other hand, how many of my classmates were able to shop in Saks? Without worrying about the price? The amount of money I was to carry made me feel dizzy.

The next afternoon, when I returned home from school, I ate a quick snack and called Ricky.

"Nu, can you come?" I asked impatiently.

"Yes, I can," she sounded really excited. I wondered how she got her mother to agree.

"Okay, I'll pick you up in a few minutes," I said. "Bye now."

"G'bye."

Butch honked outside, and I turned to go. "Bye, now, and have a safe trip," said Jenny, trying to smile. "And have mazel with the outfit," gushed Susan, almost as excited as me.

We picked up Ricky and the two of us giggled all

the way to the department store. Butch dropped us off right at the door, and arranged to meet us two hours later.

"Wow, such door-to-door service," said Ricky, overawed.

"That's what happens when you live with a rich aunt and uncle," I flippantly replied, realizing, too late, that she might be hurt. But Ricky took the comment in stride, as she did everything else.

Ricky looked a little dowdy in a plaid blouse and navy skirt stretched over her ample figure. At least her hair was neatly brushed and her shirttails were tucked in. I wished she would pay more attention to her appearance, until I reminded myself that a few months ago, I was the "*nebach* case" who dressed in old hand-me-downs and always looked *shlumpy*. Oh, well! I guess I had changed a lot after all.

It was good that Ricky was so easy-going, I reflected, or else she would be embarrassed to be part of such a one-sided friendship, where I did most of the giving.

"Good afternoon, ladies, may I help you?" asked a perfectly groomed saleswoman, smiling at us condescendingly.

"Yes, uh, I'm looking for an elegant dress, something I can wear to a special party," I began.

"Come this way," she pointed. "You want women's evening wear."

We followed her carefully, our eyes drinking it all

in—the elegant decor, the decorative fixtures, the luxurious array of linens and cosmetics, ensembles and outerwear. Finally, we arrived at the women's evening wear section.

"What size are you?" the saleslady asked.

I was surprised she was taking us seriously, two teenaged girls alone on a shopping spree. Either she was trained to be polite, or else she had a sixth sense that told her we were serious buyers. Salespeople usually pick up on these cues early on.

"I'm a teen's twelve, which would make me a ladies' two or four," I replied, luckily remembering from when I shopped with Aunt Shifra.

"Look through these racks, and pick out anything you'd like to try on. The dressing room's over there."

And pick I did. Disregarding the price tags, which were outrageous, I went through the racks and selected anything that looked promising.

"I can't believe this is happening to me," I said to Ricky, my arms loaded with clothes. "I was the shlumpiest kid in my school back home. My mother picked our stuff up in bazaars and secondhand shops. And now I'm actually shopping in one of the most expensive stores in town!"

Since Ricky still had to buy stuff in bazaars, she knew exactly what I meant. "Had someone told you, a year ago, that this would be happening to you, would you have believed her?"

"Never!" I said with conviction, as we walked to the fitting room, staggering under our load.

"Wow, you look like a different person," Ricky marveled when I tried on something really stunning. "I mean, not that you didn't look good until now," she corrected herself, blushing. We stood in front of the mirror, inspecting, complimenting, and criticizing.

"Well, I'm glad you added that," I kidded, trying on a dress I was sure my aunt would think was elegant. I pirouetted about in the wide velvet skirt, eliciting quite a few stares from the other patrons. I didn't care. I had to admit, the green silk bodice looked great with my red hair and freckled face and gave me a mature, sophisticated air.

"So, are you taking it?" Ricky inquired in a timid voice. "Did you look at the price tag?" I did. It was outrageous. But my aunt had told me that I could spend as much as $200 if I had to. I felt guilty buying it, but not as guilty as I would have felt a few months earlier, when I had first arrived. Had the wealth spoiled me so?

Watching me, Ricky admitted that she wished she could lose weight and wear prettier clothes. I would have loved to buy her an outfit, but I hadn't yet asked my aunt. I promised to loan her the skirt and top the day she could fit into it.

"My, Leah, what good taste you have," Aunt Beth beamed, when I returned home and showed off my purchase. It was late and I was exhausted after the shopping trip, but thrilled by her response. I could see that she was trying so hard to be nice to me. It would take me a little longer to warm up to her.

"So I was right about trusting her judgement, wasn't I?" asked Uncle Gerald. Aunt Beth didn't reply. She looked strained lately, and I wondered whether it was work or something else. I had a feeling the Steins were hiding something from me, something that had to do with their protectiveness, with their fear of letting me go places alone. It had also been strange how Aunt Beth worried about me risking my health. It wasn't anything I could put my finger on, just something I felt. But I kept my thoughts to myself.

Tuesday evening, the night of their anniversary, I dressed carefully. The dress fit me like a glove, and together with my new suede Shabbos shoes, I looked like a spoiled, rich kid. The lighting was dimmed, with two candles majestically casting elongated shadows on the elegant linen tablecloth. The table was set with the best china dishes, and the food, well, what a spread! Susan bustled about, carving the meat and bringing more napkins. I barely ate anything, wary of staining my stunning new dress, and cast surreptitious glances at Jenny, who sat across from me, eating. Mr. and Mrs. Stein were reminiscing quietly, their whispers traveling over the table. With a start, I realized how quiet and empty this large house was when there were no guests, and gave a happy shudder.

When the meal was over, Susan surprised us with an amazing dessert! The seven-layer pareve ice cream cake was covered with tiny, wild strawberries, and looked like it came straight out of Candyland.

"Mmm...delicious!" said Uncle Gerald, so unlike his usual, staid self. He usually didn't compliment the food, being too absorbed in his thoughts.

"Susan, you've really outdone yourself. I hope you don't plan on serving such delicious desserts while we're away!" Aunt Beth joked.

"Away?" I asked, confused.

"I'm sorry I haven't mentioned it before," said Aunt Beth, turning to me. We had planned this a year ago. Uncle Gerald and I will be leaving for a week's vacation tomorrow—an anniversary vacation."

"Can I have half the week off?" Susan asked unexpectedly, standing by the dining room door. "There's lots of food in the freezer, enough to last all week."

The Steins looked at each other, silently deliberating. Finally, Aunt Beth spoke.

"I don't see why not," she said slowly, looking to her husband to see if he agreed. "You certainly deserve a vacation. Think you can manage on your own, Jenny?"

Jenny nodded slowly.

Suddenly, I felt slightly dizzy, and also exhilarated. Too much was happening at once! What would it be like to spend one week all on my own? Well, practically on my own. There was one sour note to my unexpected freedom—Jenny. She was sure to spoil the grand plans that suddenly went through my head. Staying up late with library books! Talking on the phone until all hours! Going to Ricky's and hanging out there until late! I glanced at her, and saw (or did I?) the hint of a smile hovering about her lips. I winked at her in an impulsive gesture but she looked away. Would I be able to tolerate a week alone with her?

The Steins left early the next morning. From the sweet semi-consciousness of my dream world, I heard Butch honk as hurried footsteps clattered downstairs. Then all was quiet, and I drifted back into a blissful sleep.

That day, when I arrived home from school, no one was in the house. No one, that is, except Jenny, who was waiting with a cup of chocolate milk.

"Hello, Leah," she said awkwardly.

"Hello," I replied.

We sized each other up. How would this week turn out? Would we get along?

"How was your day?" she asked carefully.

"Fine, *boruch Hashem.* Jenny, is it okay if I call my sister now? It should be just before her bedtime."

"Go right ahead," said Jenny.

Malky and I spent a half hour laughing, shmoozing and making plans for our time together. It was amazing speaking to her—a breath of fresh air.

"That was quite a long conversation," Jenny remarked.

"Yes, and I'm sorry," I guiltily conceded. "It must have costed a fortune."

"Cost, not costed," Jenny corrected. "But don't worry about it—the Steins gave you permission. You've been speaking to her pretty often lately, although when you first arrived, you didn't call her for a long time," she commented. Wow, was she observant!

"That's true, but I should have. Maybe she would have been happier." Jenny nodded understandingly, as I continued. "You see, she thought that I was so happy in my new home that I had forgotten about her. And though she mentioned how miserable she was in one of her letters, I thought that everything had been straightened out, and that she had become so happy she had forgotten about me!"

"So each of you felt abandoned by the other, right?" Jenny asked softly, so unlike her usual prickly, bossy self. I sensed the subtle change in atmosphere, and inched closer to the table.

"This only proves my old belief," Jenny reiterated. "Families should stay together, or at least stay in touch often."

"How long have you been living here?" I asked, feeling that Jenny was ready to be my friend.

Maybe this time Jenny would tell me her mysterious story. Every time I had previously asked her questions about where she was from she had changed the subject.

"Oh, it's a couple of years now since Beth hired me. But although I manage her house, she's more like a mother to me." Her voice broke but only for an instant. Her inborn self-control took over as she continued.

"Your aunt has a heart of gold. Mr. and Mrs. Stein are two of the nicest people I've ever known. You don't appreciate them, Leah." That last statement was said as an accusation and I hastened to defend myself.

The words came out in a torrent. "That's all right for you to say," I broke in. "You work here and practically run the house for my aunt. I am the poor, homeless girl she took in. Although she's been much kinder to me lately, I still feel like I'm walking a tightrope under her critical eye. She wants me to live up to some perfect image and it's just too hard! I'm just a normal girl!"

Jenny looked straight at me, and I stared into her blue eyes, finding them somewhat softened by our shared confidences.

"Leah, I hope you don't mind my saying this, but I don't think you understand the meaning of the word appreciation. Since you've come here, you've been more of a taker than a giver. When are you going to realize that one also has to be a giver?"

I stood rooted to my place in shock. What was Jenny saying? Then I stammered, "a taker?"

"And a pretty disgruntled one at that. You think the Steins took you in just to do your Uncle Michael a favor, or because they pitied you? How can you be so blind? They are aching to impart some love, but you won't let yourself be loved. Did it ever enter your mind to make an attempt to make them happy in return? To really *try* to like it here?"

I was surprised. Maybe I had been selfish. But I was just a kid! How could I know what the Steins wanted from me?

"I don't know, Jenny, I guess I never thought about what the Steins wanted," I replied, chastened, stunned by her directness.

It's funny how one little comment can change things. Once I admitted that Jenny had a point, I sensed a dramatic softening in her attitude.

"Believe me, I know what I'm talking about," she said. "You think that I'm a strict-faced sourpuss, always giving orders and telling you what to do. You don't really know me. Not many people do."

I stared at her, intrigued by her words. There was certainly a lot more to Jenny than what met the eye. I knew that she was opening up and I would finally find out what brought her to this house.

"I lost both my parents when I was very little," she continued, almost whispering. "In fact, I never had the privilege of knowing them. For as long as I can remember, I lived in an orphanage or with a foster family. It wasn't a happy life. I won't go into all the details because they are too painful. The Steins hired me to help around the house a couple of years ago, and I've been here ever since. Beth has truly been like a mother to me, and I can really say that this is the only place that I can truly call home."

Suddenly, I thought I understood Jenny's bossiness. Sometimes, I too was also really bossy and secretive—like with Ricky. It was just a way of not letting anyone get too close to me.

"How old are you, Jenny?" I asked, shocked at my own impudence.

Jenny seemed lost in thought. But she smiled at me and said, "I'm going to be twenty-eight next June."

Wow. She was younger than I thought. I thought she was much older.

We sat together, each sunk in our own thoughts, as the kitchen clock ticked the minutes away.

"Jenny, can I ask you a question?" I said, on the spur of the moment.

"Yes?" she guardedly replied.

"Why is my aunt so protective? She doesn't want me to go anywhere alone, and she's so afraid that something will happen to me. It just doesn't make any sense!"

Jenny didn't reply. She sat there, thinking, probably wondering what to say.

"Is it a secret?" I pressed on. "something I'm not supposed to know about?"

"Well, it isn't really a secret, but nobody talks about it. You'll never hear the Steins mentioning a word of it, not even when they're alone," Jenny said. "They want to forget about what happened, like it never existed. But I don't think that's healthy. You can't heal if you don't relive the past."

By now I was really intrigued. "What happened?" I almost shouted. "Please tell me!"

Jenny looked at me, her eyes clouded with tears. "The Steins, your aunt and uncle, have a married son living in Europe." I nodded, aware of that. Their son was an independent sort, and he and his wife didn't call much. They had no children yet.

"Their son, Boruch, wasn't their only child," Jenny continued, speaking in a whisper, even though there was no one to overhear us. "They once had another child, a little girl...."

"And? What happened?" I asked, a sinking feeling in the pit of my stomach. I remembered the photo I had come upon in the drawer weeks earlier.

"The Steins have another home in Belgium, where they go frequently on business. Many years ago, when their little girl was about eight, they were in Belgium on a business trip. Their children stayed in America, with a babysitter. One afternoon, on her way home from school, the little girl, Devorah, was hit by a car."

"That's terrible!" I said tears forming in my eyes. "Did she..." I couldn't bring myself to finish.

"She went into a coma, and was in the hospital for many months," Jenny continued. "It was a tragic, long illness. Finally, she passed away about a year after the accident, and things haven't been the same since."

"*Nebach*!" I said, horrified. "how they must have suffered!"

Jenny nodded. "I wasn't working for them then, but from what I gather, the tragedy affected them deeply. Especially your aunt. She's been a changed person since then. Very bitter and withdrawn, and enormously protective of her son. He couldn't tolerate her overprotectiveness, and went to Israel to yeshiva as soon as he was old enough. Now he's married and has his own life."

"And the Steins are left with an empty house," I continued. It was all so sad.

"An empty house, and you. One moody teenager to love, to somehow take the place of their own daughter."

"But I'll never take their daughter's place!" I protested.

"You won't," Jenny replied, "but you have a place of your own in their hearts."

"Now I realize who that girl was!" I said, without thinking.

"Which girl?" asked Jenny suspiciously.

"Oh, nothing, I was just thinking aloud," I replied. Jenny shrugged, and got up to do her chores.

After that conversation, I didn't have much appetite for supper. I silently did some homework, and went to bed an hour early.

Sleep eluded me. I had a lot to think about that night. Now I realized why Aunt Beth was so obsessed with responsibility. She probably never recovered from her daughter's death. Maybe she even felt guilty. Who knows? Although I still didn't understand her preoccupation with perfect grades, clothes and external impressions, I did understand her better.

Of one thing I was certain. I never wanted to be called a taker by Jenny or by anyone else. I would try to repay the Steins—not with money, of course, but by doing something that would make them happy with me, by showing them that they hadn't made a mistake by taking me in. I would throw myself into my studies, make friends with all my classmates, and please my aunt by even having my friends over and showing her that I appreciated the school she had taken the time to choose for me, and that I was really making an effort to get along at school.

"Jenny?" I called out over the intercom, forgetting it was way past midnight.

"Huh?" she sleepily replied. "What is it?"

"Jenny, can I have a sleepover party?"

Sleepover Party

riday. I walked into the class-room slowly, carefully lugging a bag filled with twenty-five invitations. After we had spoken by telephone to the Steins and they had happily agreed, Jenny and I had worked on the invitations all Thursday evening.

Miss Rina Leah Berger would like to
cordially invite you to attend a sleepover party,
10 p.m. Motzei Shabbos at 18 Elm Place.
Come and bring your ruach!

As the girls filed out to recess, I stayed behind, placing an invitation on every girl's desk. When my classmates returned and saw the stunning envelopes, they hurried to their desks, many of them ripping the envelopes open in their excitement. It was interesting to hear the different reactions.

"Wow, Leah! These invitations are gorgeous!"

"A sleepover party! What's the occasion?"

"Leah, are you for real? You're sure your aunt won't mind?"

"Sure, I'm sure. And there doesn't have to be an occasion to have a party, does there?"

"No, of course not," Yocheved hastened to reply. "It's just that usually sleepover parties are for birthdays or something."

"Well, if you must know, this is for a happy occasion. My birthday is coming up in a few weeks, but that's not the reason for the party." My voice trailed off; I was uncertain of what else to say.

"I have a good reason!" chimed in Zahava. "This party is purely for fun." She rubbed her hands together as her hazel eyes glittered with excitement. "I'm sure we'll have a blast!"

"Right on!" Yael chimed in. "That sounds more like it." Some other girls nodded in agreement. "You don't need a reason to make a party!"

There was a babble of voices as the girls excitedly debated the merits of a sleepover party, and how exciting it would be to stay up all night in the grandest house in town.

Dina wasn't in school that day, but that didn't

bother me too much. Since I had come back to school she hadn't been too friendly. Maybe she felt badly about what had happened. I knew I should talk to her, but it was one of the things I kept pushing off. One day...

Only Ricky seemed subdued as she sat in her seat, munching on a brownie. Without even speaking to her, I already knew what was going through her mind.

"Hiya Ricky, what's new?" I made my way to my seat and dug into the delicious chocolate cake that Ricky baked every week.

She shrugged.

"You're mad at me, right?" I asked.

Another shrug.

"Ricky, don't do that to me, pleeease! I don't understand sign language, and I can't risk losing my *best friend* either!" I stressed the words "best friend". "So let's talk, okay?"

I saw her expression relax, and her grumpy features seemed to warm up a little.

"I'm not mad at you, honest. It's just that I thought that since you invited everyone to the party and I'm just a plain dumb girl, you wouldn't want to bother with me anymore!"

"Oh, Ricky," I replied, too upset to notice that the math teacher was standing by the door. "Ricky, no matter how many new or popular friends I make, you're the old friend that stood beside me through thick and thin, and I'll never forget that, *bli neder*," I reassured her, and my voice rose. "Besides, I have another reason for making this party."

"Did I hear something about a party, Leah?" asked a smooth, annoyed voice. "I want all of you to place your algebra homework on your desk, or you will have plenty of reasons not to make a party." Mrs. Sander, the math teacher, clearly meant business.

The hubbub abated, as the excited class pulled out their math books and the lesson began.

Motzei Shabbos finally arrived. In honor of the grand party, Susan returned from her vacation a day early—right after Shabbos had ended. She was supposed to have off until Sunday night, but when she called to find out how everything was going and heard about the party, she couldn't resist. I loved her for it.

Wow, did she prepare a storm! Jenny and I had ordered rolls, hot dogs and cold cuts and had them delivered before Shabbos. I hovered at the sidelines, helping her prepare. Jenny had spoken with the Steins again and they were pleased that I was having so many friends over and were sorry that they couldn't be around. The house reached a feverish pitch of excitement as I helped Jenny select the dinnerware for this occasion and set the table. In vain did I protest about the china dishes.

"It's only a get-together for teenagers. Paper plates will be just fine. What do we need china for?"

"You know that Mrs. Stein will not entertain on anything other than china!" Jenny replied. "In this home, certain standards are upheld, regardless of the age of the guests being entertained."

"All right," I finally relented. "But don't blame me if a dish accidentally crashes to the floor." I could have been a prophet. My aunt's finest china would prove to be no match for twenty-three exuberant girls.

The party started with a boom, as Chany tapped on the front door, huffing and puffing. As I opened, she staggered in with a tremendous black box.

"Wha-what have you got there?" I eyed her warily. "Are you planning to blow the house up?"

"Something like it," Chany chuckled as she pushed me aside and set the box on the floor. Only when she moved away did I see that it was an enormous portable stereo, complete with speakers. I was glad she had brought this—the Steins had a stereo, of course, but it was super expensive, and I had been warned never to touch it without Mr. Stein showing me how to use it.

"Wow! You really do know how to liven up a party!" I remarked, as she turned it on, and the music of Mordechai Ben David filled the air.

Soon the rest of the girls arrived, and we dragged the stereo downstairs to the enormous finished basement where Jenny had set up a big table. We noshed on tiny frankfurters and buns with mustard. Susan had prepared a mini deli, complete with sauerkraut, ketchup and pickles. I had asked for a "make your own deli sandwich" kind of treat and there was a choice of a huge assortment of cold cuts and cold salads. Susan had made everything look fantastic!

We shmoozed and stuffed ourselves until we were full. When the games we had prepared were dutifully played, I winked significantly at Chany, who quietly slunk away. Suddenly, a loud boom made us jump. The room became full of loud simcha music as, one by one, we formed a circle and danced. Round and round the table we went, until a couple of china dishes actually crashed onto the floor. Finally, exhausted girls dropped out one by one, until only a few super *lebedig* girls remained in the circle. I sprawled on a chair, spent, watching Ricky grin at me as she kept up the jump, skip, hop, her breath coming in shallow gasps. By now, only she and Chany were left, and with sweaty faces they danced arm in arm, like two entertainers. Everyone cheered them along.

"Faster, Ricky!"

"Let's go, Chany. Give it all you've got!"

"C'mon girls!"

And then there was a loud "Hurray!" as the two held on tightly and careened about for a final spin. The spin ended with their collapse on the floor and a few good-natured attempts at reviving the fallen entertainers. I marveled at how Ricky had changed.

Though she was wearing plain dress, her face glowed with excitement and she seemed more confident.

"Okay, time to clear out," I cheerfully announced. "I think Jenny wants to get rid of the mess over here."

"We can help her," one of the girls offered, as others in the noisy group drifted to the back of the large basement where Jenny had prepared blankets and pillows. Girls were lying about telling stories and laughing.

"Oh, no, thank you. Susan and I can do it on our own," Jenny dismissed them.

"Y...you're sure?" Dina timidly asked, looking as if she wouldn't mind being excused from her offer.

"After all," joked Jenny, "I wouldn't want to risk any more broken china!" Jenny and Susan made it clear that we weren't to help and so we trooped toward the back of the finished basement, which was large and comfy. Most girls had brought their own sleeping bags, and were now busy setting everything up and choosing their corners on the thickly padded carpet. Other girls were preparing for bed in the upstairs bathrooms or the one in the basement.

"Ready for bed, anyone?" I ventured.

"Bed? Did you invite us here to sleep?" Yocheved protested, indignantly. "A bed I can have in my own house. I came here to have fun. Ditto, anyone?"

There was a roar of approval at this.

"What's a sleepover party for, anyway?" Rachel wanted to know, her cute ponytail bouncing as she grinned mischievously. "Isn't it to stay up all night and have a grand time?"

"Oh, and I always thought it was for showing off our robes, silly!" Yael answered her. Everyone burst out laughing.

"Now that I think about it, isn't there a special reason you made a pajama party?" Zahava asked. Seeing the look of panic that crossed my face, she hastened to add, "I mean, remember what you began saying when Mrs. Sander walked in on you."

"Boy, was that funny!" Chany cut in sarcastically. "She sure does have a great sense of humor."

"*Loshon hora*," two girls sang out. There was a moment of strained silence.

"Anyway," practical Yael began, scrunching her face in an attempt to look serious. "*What* is the reason for this party?"

"Okay. Here goes," I said abruptly. "The reason for the sleepover party is—"

"To have fun!" Zahava blurted out. "And to eat amazing food, and schmooze with your friends, and..."

"And to play games, and have pillow fights, like this!" laughed Yocheved, throwing a pillow at Rachel. The fun began. Pillows flew into the air, landing in the weirdest places.

Jenny had picked this particular moment to poke her head around the stairway leading into the game room. She looked alarmed, yet amused—as if she wanted to throw us all out, yet enjoyed our romping.

"Oh, Jenny, we're so sorry!" I burst out. "Nobody meant to do any harm."

"Don't worry about it," Jenny replied. "After all, this is your night to have fun! If you can't have fun when you're a teenager, when can you have fun?"

The girls were amazed at Jenny's attitude, and there was much discussion about the accommodating housekeeper. Yet even Jenny had to take second place to Susan, who brought down glasses of hot tea, warm cinnamon buns, and bags of candy to add the perfect touch to the final activity, a class *kumzits*.

Shany played the old basement piano and Yael and Yocheved harmonized. It was exhilarating, moving, and uplifting—definitely something I wouldn't have missed for the world. And yet, if not for my uncle's understanding words, I would have been too afraid to tell anyone about myself and would've never felt like I belonged! I suddenly felt so amazingly grateful that my aunt and uncle had given me this chance to have a normal life. I mean while we were singing, for the first time since my mother's illness, I felt as if the cloud over my life had moved on.

I had never gotten a chance to explain why I'd made the sleepover party but the fun and camaraderie of these girls I could now call my friends were reason enough. One by one girls crawled into their sleeping bags. The conversation was filled with merry, lively debates from groups of girls huddled on the huge carpeted game room floor. But after a while, shouts simmered down to whispers, and little by little, conversation was replaced by snores and by the kind of comments that happen when a bunch of girls sleep on the floor of a basement.

"Ouch! Get your elbow out of my face!"

"Ich! There's a pair of feet right near my nose!"

"Hey, I'm sitting on someone's glasses!"

"OOOOh (stretch) what time is it?"

"OW! You knocked your hands into my nose!"

"Could you be quiet already!" (tremendous yawn).

One by one the sleepy, overtired girls yawned and mumbled as they turned over on the thick blue carpet and fell asleep.

Morning. We were all exhausted, trying to shut out the warm rays of the early morning sun peeping through the blinds. The adventurous amongst my classmates were already up and involved in a heated conversation in one corner, occasionally interrupted by the mumbled complaints and plaintive "let-me-sleeps!" coming from the majority of girls still curled up.

I woke slowly, stretching lazily, almost hitting Dina in the face. Studious, quiet Dina had dropped off beside me, and now was snoring slightly. I gave her an experimental shove.

"Hmm...mmm..." she mumbled, and turned to her other side. By then I was wide awake.

I ran to the sink, washed *negel vasser*, said *Modeh Ani* and wiped the sleep from my eyes. Then I raced upstairs to find Susan. There's nothing like a hot cup of chocolate and some fresh cinnamon buns at 8:30 in the morning. As my dressing gown trailed after me on the stairs, I anticipated Susan already dressed in her cap and apron, and the delicious brew prepared, its steam wafting over the cheery kitchen. But the kitchen was still dark. It was still early for a Sunday morning.

Disappointed, I went back down the stairs empty-handed. Rachel was the first to notice me, coming down the stairs. "Where's the hot chocolate you promised you were bringing?"

"Oh, that was a nice welcome you just gave her!" teased Chany. "Actually, I wouldn't mind a cup of coffee myself."

"Coffee! You drink coffee?" Ricky said, incredulous.

"Why not? What's wrong with coffee?" asked Yocheved. "My mother lives on it."

"So does mine, but I wouldn't go near the nasty,

bitter brew!" interjected Dina, well known for her original outbursts.

"Um, actually, I went up to get some hot drinks and danishes," I began. I noticed some girls licking their lips. "But the kitchen was dark, and Susan is still asleep. It's a little early for them to get up!"

"So what's the problem?" said Yocheved. "We don't have to bother anyone! We can prepare it ourselves."

"I'm not really so sure," I began lamely, wondering whether it was a good idea to let twenty-three active girls into Susan's immaculate kitchen. "I don't really know where anything is."

"What do you mean, you don't know? The coffee and cocoa are probably in the cupboard, the water is in the kettle, and the dishes are in the cabinet. So let's go eat upstairs."

"Yeah, right. You know what, why don't we all get dressed?" piped up Shany. Quick as a mouse, she was already burrowing into her clothes under her sleeping bag, coming up occasionally for air. "I'm halfway dressed already, so I'll help you prepare the drinks and stuff, and then when the other girls are ready, they'll come up." We all laughed at Shany every time she surfaced from under the blanket.

Joking and shmoozing, Chany, Shany and I made our way upstairs. Most of the other girls still seemed dead to the world. We could surprise them all with a great big breakfast.

When we got upstairs we were surprised to find the kitchen lights were on. Susan stood in the middle of the room, looking tired, wearing her familiar apron, as she stacked rows of danishes onto trays.

"Morning, Susan!" I sang out. "Were you able to sleep with all this noise?" "Well, actually," she said, "you girls kept me up until 4:00 a.m. with all your talking. That's why I am late in getting up!"

"Oh, Susan, I'm so sorry!" I burst out, giving her a hug. Chany looked on, startled, as Susan hugged me back. I guess she thought of Susan as the kitchen help, while I considered her like another aunt or something.

"Well now, that's okay. We don't have a party here every night! Did you have a good time?"

"We sure did!" Chany and Shany assured her.

"Well, that's the main thing," Susan replied. "Now, call the girls up for a munch."

"Breakfast!" Chany called down.

"Wait, we're not all dressed yet!" came the plaintive cry from downstairs. So the three of us munched for a minute on the fragrant warm cinnamon buns. I heard the click of Jenny's heels and turned to greet her. She was immaculately dressed, yet she looked tired. Did we disturb her sleep too? I felt awfully guilty. I never imagined that they would hear our noise from the basement to the third floor!

"Good morning girls," she greeted us warmly. "Breakfast will be ready in an hour. Actually, you probably won't be able to eat much breakfast after your snack!"

Finally, all twenty-three of us were dressed, davened, and had somewhat straightened up the basement. By then the clock read nine thirty, and breakfast was prepared.

Breakfast consisted of steaming plates of scrambled eggs, fresh warm rolls and bagels, a vegetable salad and, of course, luscious cinnamon buns, danishes and hot chocolate. We ate heartily, and it was an extremely merry, tired group of girls that morning at the Steins. Soon, the phones began to ring off the hook as parents arranged pick up times for the girls. By eleven thirty everyone, including Chany and her tremendous stereo system, was gone. I felt on top of the world, on cloud nine! I belonged!

The Attic

uesday afternoon. I walked up the front path of the Stein's house, humming. A glance at the driveway told me the Steins weren't back yet. Oh, well. By now I missed them a tiny bit, even though I couldn't bring myself to admit it. I shivered in the cold, wiping my boots on the outdoor mat.

I opened the front door with my key, shook the accumulated snowflakes off my coat, and stepped into the elegant foyer. It was crowded, strewn with luggage and boxes.

"Hi! I'm home!" I announced to Jenny. "What's all this about?" I asked curiously.

"The Steins arrived home about an hour ago,

dropped their luggage, and went straight to their office to pick up the mail and check on the paperwork. They also mentioned an important meeting," said Jenny, distracted.

Then she turned back to Susan, who looked slightly miffed. "Are you sure the warranty is in the attic?"

"If I remember correctly, that's where Mrs. Stein said it's supposed to be."

"We need to return the garment bag to the company," continued Susan, smiling at me, "because it's all torn. See?" she pointed to a large rip in the seam. "I called the luggage company, and explained that since the luggage is covered under a five-year guarantee, and it's an expensive piece, we would like to exchange it as soon as possible."

"Are you going to bring it down?" Jenny asked, looking uncomfortable.

"Me? Bring it down? You know I can't climb all those stairs constantly with my bad knees! You've always said you don't mind the stairs!" Susan said, looking at Jenny.

"Mrs. Stein asked you to take care of it," said Jenny.

That's interesting, I thought. It's usually Jenny's job to take care of these things. Susan only does the cooking.

"I am not tramping up there," said Susan, her face red with anger. I saw she was struggling to control herself. I wanted to prevent a fight, so I spoke up.

"I'll go," I said, startling Jenny.

"You? Why, the very thing. The attic is old and musty; three flights up. You can only go up there through a dark stairway. The stairs are dusty, and you can slip."

"It's okay. I'm old enough to go up there myself," I assured her, smiling at Susan. I think both of them were relieved to be spared the trip, and the quarrel.

"Okay, if you say so," said Jenny, while Susan flashed me the "thumbs up" sign. I trooped up to the second floor, past my bedroom, and went up still another flight of stairs.

I passed Susan's and Jenny's bedrooms and an old, empty room that I had never seen before. Then I turned a corner and came face to face with a wooden door.

I used the key Jenny had given me. I craned my neck, peering through the semi-darkness up an old, rickety flight of stairs. It was a dark and musty world up there, none too inviting.

"Remember, now. The original box the luggage came in is supposed to be along a wall. The warranty should be inside. The light switch is on your left," Jenny had told me. I made my way up the stairs, groping in the darkness like a blind person.

I reached the landing, my hand blindly grabbing

at the wall for a few seconds, looking for a light switch. I brushed against it, and a feeble light filled the musty room. Before me was the Stein's attic, in all its glory. The room was medium-sized, with a low ceiling, crumbly floorboards and unpainted walls. In contrast to the spotless mansion below, this room was in complete disarray. It looked like one of the messy thrift shops my Mom used to take me to.

There were boxes of every size and description scattered about. Antique wooden trunks were piled up in the corners. I wondered what was inside? Old racks were filled with plastic-wrapped clothing, smelling sharply from mothballs. It took me a few moments to locate the box, and I stuck my hand inside. I found an envelope and pulled it out. I had found it! The warranty was in my hand. Mission accomplished.

I turned to go, when I impulsively decided to linger. "What if there is a buried treasure hidden somewhere?" an illogical voice inside me asked. As an avid reader of mystery books, I couldn't resist the lure of an unexplored attic.

I opened the first trunk, and saw more clothes, pairs of strangely shaped shoes and ridiculous hats. This would be great for Purim, I thought. I was sure this didn't all belong to my aunt. The previous owner probably left her storage; the clothing certainly looked used.

There was another trunk, behind this one, much smaller in size. I opened it, wondering if there were any more clothes. Nope. Just some papers and legal documents. I reached for the pile instinctively, forgetting where I was, that these papers didn't belong to me, and that perhaps I had no right to read them.

Most of the documents looked like they concerned business deals, especially real estate. Perhaps the previous owner had been an agent...But no. There were the names, Gerald and Beth Stein, clearly written on one document.

I searched a few more moments, coming upon a stack of old letters. There were some bills, wedding invitations, letters...I flipped through them, and froze. There, on the bottom of the pile, was a letter, written in a familiar handwriting.

Astonishingly familiar. There were a few similar letters underneath. They were all addressed to Mrs. Beth Stein. The first letter of every word was written in bold, capital letters, while the rest of the name and address was scrawled in script. I would have recognized the handwriting in my dreams.

I replaced the rest of the pile, grabbed the letters I wanted, and stuck them into my skirt pocket. Then I closed the light, feeling my way down the stairs, warranty in hand.

The familiar sunlight of the third floor filled the room. I blinked.

"What took you so long?" Jenny asked, peering at

me sharply while I handed her the warranty. Perhaps she suspected I was hiding something.

I shrugged, mumbled something about taking some time to find the box, and walked down the stairs to my room. I needed to be alone.

I waited until Jenny's footsteps on the landing told me she had reached the first floor, and then I locked my door. Sitting down at my desk, I felt my hands shaking. I put the letters on the desk, all five of them. Which one should I read first? They were all air mail envelopes, addressed to the Steins, at an address in Belgium. Hmm...that makes sense. Aunt Shifra had told me the Steins had a home overseas as well. But I thought they lived mainly in New York. Oh, I guess things were different fifteen years ago. That would explain these letters. It probably was expensive to call. Where should I start?

Wait, let me see the postmarks. I squinted to read the dates on the letters; I could barely figure them out. Let's see what we've got here. I fingered them gingerly. The oldest one was written fifteen years ago, two years before I was born.

With shaking fingers, I opened the envelope, and withdrew a plain, creased sheet of paper. I opened it, and stared at the smudged print filling the lines.

Mommy! I whispered the word reverently. Mommy. Mommy. My very own mother, whose voice I had difficulty recalling and whose face was beginning to be a blur, had written these letters. Her

handwriting made it all come back, her gentle
expression, her soft voice, the way she smiled at
me. I sat immobile, not daring to read the letters.
What secrets were contained inside? Would I find
out things that would change the way I looked at
things, thought about things, treated the Steins?
Would I discover some awful secret that everyone
had tried to hide from me? Would all the puzzles I
had in my mind, about why Aunt Shifra and Uncle
Michael were so estranged from the Steins, be
solved?

Well, there was only one way to find out. Taking
a deep breath, I began to read.

Dear Beth,

*It took me a long time to respond to your let-
ter. Your accusations hurt me to the core. Yes,
Beth, I know you care for me, and want to see
me happy, but how can you say anything when
you haven't met Tzvi? He's good, kindhearted,
has midos tovos—in short he's a mentch. Don't
you understand? You've always empathized
with me. I need a fun-loving person to teach me
to enjoy life. I've had my share of suffering, as
you well know. I want to forget the sad days,
the loneliness, the years of crying into my pillow. I want to start anew. I know we've had
hard times and misunderstandings in the past,
and you're not on speaking terms with Shifra,
but I want to clear the air, and continue the spe-*

cial friendship we enjoy.

Beth, by the time you read this, Tzvi and I will be planning our wedding, which will take place on September 10, G-d willing. Yes, our engagement is by now official. I sent you a telegram, but have not received one in response. Don't be too angry with me, Beth, please! Try to understand. You are a happily married mother of two adorable children, Boruch and Devorah. Your home is filled with happy sounds, with the voices of children at play. And I am here alone, working at my office, returning home every evening to solitude and discontent. When I met Tzvi, it was as if the sun began to shine again. He has a steady job, and we rented a small apartment not too far from his office.

Beth, dear, can't you find it in your heart to be happy for me? Won't you understand? It would mean so much for me to have you and Gerald at our wedding. Please don't bear a grudge, because I didn't listen to your advice. My wedding won't be the same without you there.

P.S. I know it's hard for Gerald to leave his business contacts in Belgium, and for you to leave the children. But I'm still praying that you'll attend.

I'm sending this letter with hope in my heart

*and a prayer on my lips. Please respond at
your earliest convenience.*

Love, Brenda

Whew! What a letter! So Aunt Beth didn't want
Mommy to marry Daddy! She probably realized
what Mommy didn't, that they had never been suit-
ed to each other.

I was dying to know what happened in the end.
Did Aunt Beth come to the wedding? I had a sink-
ing feeling in my heart. What did it matter anyway?
It was history, the events took place before I was
born, and had no bearing on my present situation.
But I still wanted to know….

I shook my head to dispel these thoughts and
opened the second letter. This one had no date; the
postmark was too smudgy to read. Oh, well.

Dearest Beth,

*I hope that this letter finds you in perfect
health, and that your children are doing fine.
Do you have more time on your hands now that
both children are spending a good part of the
day in school? How are the educational standards in the European schools? Are they up to
par? You mentioned something about Gerald's
new business venture. Does your degree in
educational psychology help him in any way?
Will his partner in Belgium agree to let him run
his end of things in the States? Which brings
me to my next question:*

Are you planning to come back to New York soon? You mentioned something about buying a big house in the suburbs and renovating it. I'd love to have you live a little closer to me to be able to call more frequently. It's so much easier to pick up the phone than to write a letter.

Enough questions for now. Here's some news from my angle. I know you love to hear news about the children, as much as I love writing about their antics. Rina Leah, my mature five-and-a-half-year old, loves to dress up in Mommy's clothes. She is such a pretty child, and reminds me of my mother, Leah, a"h. Though I like the name Rina, I try to call her Rina Leah, to keep my mother's memory alive. Four-year-old Malky is my dreamer, and enjoys curling up with her collection of dollies and an old blankie to cover them. (Hmmm...were we really once like that?)

The kids are growing nicely, thank G-d. Money is still tight since Tzvi lost his job, but I'm not complaining. I have my children, and that's all that counts. Thank you for offering to pay for our tickets and have us visit you, but I'm afraid we won't be able to swing it just now. The children are young and it's hard to make such a long journey. Tzvi's still looking for a job, and we're all going through hard times. I do hope you'll save us a raincheck, for when the kids are older.

In the meantime, I miss you, Gerald, and the children. Has it really been four years since we last saw each other, when you came to Malky's kiddush? She's a little lady already, with love- ly blonde hair. Leah's hair is bright red and I think it's gorgeous.

I think I'll sign off for now. So tired. The kids wake me up at 6:00 a.m.

Love,

Your dearest Brenda

I didn't reach for the third letter right away. First I needed to think. I reached back into the recesses of my memory, trying to recall an old conversation. It happened when Mommy was sick, and she was on the phone a lot, with doctors and concerned friends.

I recalled Mommy talking a lot to someone who was then in Europe—a rich friend, but no, closer than a friend. I think she was something like a sur- rogate mother. Her name was Beth, that much I gathered from the conversations. Apparently, this Beth wanted to come and take care of us, but Mommy refused. "You've already done so much for me, for all of us," she said. "Where would we have been without you? Three fatherless children, stuck in Russia?"

There was some conversation, and then Mommy said something like, "I'll never forget what you did for us then. Shifra and David were too young to recall—all they remember is the trip to America with our mother. But I remember how you paid for our tickets and arranged for our visas. And what you did for us after we arrived, setting up our apartment and buying us groceries..." Mommy's voice became nostalgic.

When she hung up I asked, "Who was that?"

"An old family friend," she said, distracted. "More than a friend. If not for her and her parents, we might have starved in Russia. There was nothing to eat. My parents were fired from their jobs because they were Jewish. Her parents not only got us out of Russia, they actually supported us in America.

"Then why don't I hear much about her?" I asked. "Why doesn't she ever come, and why don't we go to visit her?"

"It's very complicated," Mommy replied. "Later on, after our mother died, they were very domineering. They tried to—"

Just then, the phone rang again. It was Mommy's doctor. The subject of these mysterious rich strangers was dropped, and we never had a chance to bring it up again. I never connected this with the Steins before. But now I was sure Mommy had been talking about the Steins.

Now everything made sense. Aunt Shifra's reluctance to send me here...Mommy not wanting Aunt Beth to come and take over. Mommy was probably afraid that she would be too hard on us kids. Why, then, did Aunt Beth offer to give me a home?

Suddenly, I heard a voice through the intercom, interrupting my thoughts.

"Rina?"

"Yes," I called back impatiently.

"Do you want a snack?" Susan asked.

"No, I'm studying," I fibbed. But in a sense I really was studying. I was studying the letters. "I'll be down soon."

"Fine. The Steins should be back shortly."

Uh, oh. I was definitely not in the mood to meet them this minute.

I picked up the third letter. Wow, this letter looks really blurry, filled with splotches and smudges. Could they be tear marks? And what was this? A small card fell out of the envelope. My heart skipped a beat as I read the title: condolence card.

> *Dear Beth and Gerald:*
>
> *It is with profound sympathy that we express our condolence upon the loss of your child. There are no words to describe our sorrow. May G-d comfort you amongst the mourners of Zion and Jerusalem.*
>
> *Sincerely,*
>
> *Brenda Berger*

Though Devorah had passed away years ago, the simple card made me cry in a way that the other letters hadn't. I reached for a tissue and sobbed like a baby. It was just so sad. My mother, now no longer living, writing about a little girl who had also died tragically! Life was difficult sometimes!

I don't know how much time went by, but finally I was composed enough to read the accompanying letter.

Dearest Beth,

I still haven't been able to stop crying, since the tragedy occurred. There are so many questions. Why Devorah? She was so young, so innocent, so pure. How could her life be snuffed out at eight years old by a reckless drunk driver. Why? Can we even dare ask? The Ribono Shel Olam *has His reasons. I feel your pain, as strongly as if Devorah would have been my own. How are you coping?*

I know you must be wondering why I didn't fly to Europe for the shiva, *and I am sorry to have to add more salt to your wounds. The reason I didn't fly in is because I am busy with my own problems. Tzvi and I will be divorcing in a few weeks. Beth, you were right. He is not for me and never was the right one. Oh, if only I had listened.*

You have lost your child, and I am losing my husband, through my own choice. So much pain. When will it all end?

I remain, your loving sister in sorrow, Brenda

My hands were shaking so hard I could barely continue. This was the dear, gentle mother I had known so long ago, whose memory was stirring once more in my mind. Mommy! I whispered the word reverently, feeling the longing and stab of pain that accompanied it. It felt so nice to know that Aunt Beth and Mommy were friends and that Mommy had been close to Aunt Beth. I was full of anger at Daddy, for causing Mommy so much aggravation. And poor Aunt Beth! How she must have suffered! No wonder she was so overprotective, so afraid of letting me go anywhere myself. No wonder she wanted to give me a home, perhaps she was hoping I would replace the daughter she lost. Maybe that's why she felt so tense about wanting me to excel. But Aunt Shifra hadn't let Malky and me go, until she became desperate and had to send us away. Even then, she made sure not to send us both to Aunt Beth by sending Malky to London, to her brother, and me to Aunt Beth.

Why couldn't Shifra forgive her for what happened so many years ago? I wasn't even sure what happened, but it couldn't be too serious. Then again, how would I know?

I felt like a little girl who had been sitting in the dark, trying to put a puzzle together. Little by little, the room became filled with light, as I struggled to fit the pieces in their proper place. There are only a few pieces left, and I wondered: What else is there that I do not know?

How could I have been so blind? Why didn't I pick up on the signals? Aunt Beth really did want me! If not for who I am, than to replace her daughter. But I couldn't replace anyone—just like my mother could never be replaced!

I held two more letters in my hand. Perhaps they would explain the rest of the puzzle. They looked newer than the rest, and in better condition. Good thing. My eyes were beginning to hurt from squinting.

Dearest Beth,

By now you probably have received an update on my condition from Shifra. (So they were speaking to each other after all! Maybe only because it was an emergency.) When we spoke last on the phone, I was still numb, in shock. I had barely gotten over the divorce, and was struggling to put my life together, and now this. The children are confused, not understanding what this is all about. I am also confused, frightened by all the options. I know you strongly suggest treatment through natural methods, but my doctor disagrees. I understand that you and Shifra have been communicating by phone, and some strong words were exchanged. (Aha, that makes sense.) Please don't make things harder for me by causing hard feelings. I understand that you can't come

right now because of Gerald's gallbladder sur-
gery. I know your thoughts are with me. If you
have something to say, call me directly. You
know Shifra can't handle any more pressure,
especially considering the size of her family
and her fragile nerves. If you feel uncomfortable talking to me about my illness, then write.
You know we feel comfortable corresponding
through mail. Let me hear from you. Tell me
what you think.

I think I'll end now. I'm exhausted.
(Unfortunately, I'm exhausted most of the time.)
My doctor wants to begin chemo and radiation.
I'm frightened. Ribono Shel Olam, give me
strength to handle this, to be a good mother to
my children and survive this challenge.

I'll end with a tefillah to the Healer of all
Mankind. May He hear our tefillos and wipe all
tears away.

Yours forever,
Brenda

I heard some noises outside. Without pausing to
digest the letter, I quickly opened the fifth and last,
and skimmed across the lines. The handwriting was
spidery and weak, not like the others, but still
unmistakably my mother's.

Dear Beth,
It's hard for me to write. I have no strength.
When are you coming? I hear you've finally set-

tled the European part of the business and will be staying mainly in New York. Won't you come and see me first, before...it may be too late?

No, I don't like to write these words and I'm sure you don't like to read them. Yet I must be honest. You understand what I mean. You always have. (Thank you from the bottom of my heart for the money! It has paid the rent and for all the food since my illness!)

I am trying to manage as best as I can with the children, but it's very hard. Shifra is helping as much as she can, and Rachel, David's wife, is planning to come from London, though I doubt she can stay for more than a few days. You know they have so little money and this trip would be a big expense for them. They have offered to take my children, but I refuse to part with my precious ones for even one day.

Of course, if the situation worsens, G-d forbid, then I will have no choice but to send the girls away. David and Rachel have offered to take Malky, but how can I separate my girls? I am afraid to think of what might happen if...I don't want to express the foreboding in my heart. But you understand, Beth. When it happens—if it happens—I want you to take my girls. Shifra and David won't like it, I know. They feel Malky and Rina should stay with them. They feel the families should stay togeth-

er. But you are like family, closer than family!

I trust you, Beth. I will talk to them, tell them about my wishes. Malky is fragile and delicate, but it's Rina Leah I'm concerned about. She is very much like me, so sensitive yet tough on the outside. She needs a strong hand, tempered with love.

I hope that Hashem will give me the courage to fight my illness and regain my strength so I can be a mother to my children without anyone's help. Thank you, Beth, for all your support! I don't know what I would've done without you!

With love,

Brenda

I put down the letter, utterly shaken. So many mysteries cleared up, in the span of one afternoon. I couldn't believe Mommy had wanted me to stay with her "second mother," Beth Stein and her husband. She felt they would be able to give me what I needed—a loving home, a mother and father. Adults made life so complex. I—I just wanted to be a child again, to forget about all the terrible things that had happened. And I wished more than anything now to just be with Malky. I couldn't wait for Chanukah when we would finally be together again!

Could Aunt Beth give her a home as well? I had no answer, yet. I sat and *davened* and cried, until, exhausted and spent, I could cry no more. There was so much to cry about, both happy and tragic. About my mother's death and my not knowing how close they were and why Aunt Beth was so vital to her. About my treating Aunt Beth like a stranger. About all the new people in my life and how I had begun to love everyone, even as I missed my old life.

When the volcano of feelings that had flared up quietly died down, I wiped my face and stretched out. Then I hid the letters under my mattress, changed my clothing, and brushed my hair. I had lost track of time, but suddenly I noticed it was dark outside. I heard the car pull up to the house. The Steins had arrived home, and not a moment too soon.

I watched from my window as they entered the front door, walking together, looking suddenly old and exhausted. My uncle and aunt, though not really my uncle and aunt. My guardians. They had offered me their home and their hearts, though their love was obscured by pain, having lost their own daughter. I realized, now, with a sudden clarity, that I wasn't taking the place of their daughter who had died so many years ago. I was me, Brenda's daughter—Rina Leah Berger, my very own self—and Aunt Beth was a woman like my mother, who had suffered much, yet still realized what was important in life.

I smiled when I realized the irony of what I had done. I had committed the same crime as my classmates—reading classified information. But, hopefully, the Steins would never find out. It would be my own little secret, perhaps to be shared with Malky, if the need ever presented itself.

In the meantime, I had a mission to accomplish: to clear the air between myself and the Steins who had done so much for my mother and had generously given me a chance to lead a normal life. Head held high and mind made up, I walked out of my room, no longer across the unknown, but into a new beginning.

Glossary

All of the words here are translated from the Hebrew unless noted otherwise as Yiddish (Yid.).

a"h (alav hashalom)—(lit., on him should be peace); of blessed memory

achdus—unity

aliyah—(lit., going up); immigration to Israel

amen—affirmative response to another saying a blessing

b'hatzlacha—it should be with success

bais yaakov—a girls school

bashert (Yid.)—predestined

bentched—recited the blessing made after eating bread

bezras Hashem—with G-d's help

birchas haTorah—the blessings over the Torah

bli ayin hora—without an evil eye

bli neder—without making a promise

boruch Dayan Emes—blessed is the True Judge (this blessing

277

is said after hearing that someone has passed away)

boruch Hashem (B"H)—thank G-d

bracha, brachos—blessing, blessings

bracha acharona—blessing made after eating

bubby (Yid.)—grandmother

challah—braided loaves of bread eaten on Shabbos and holidays

Chanukah chagigah—a party in honor of Chanukah

chas vesholom—G-d forbid

chesed—acts of kindness

Cheshvan, MarCheshvan—the eighth month of the Jewish calendar year, sometimes referred to as the bitter Cheshvan since in this month no Jewish holidays are celebrated

chumash—bible

churban—destruction, referring to the destruction of the holy Temple

chutzpadig—brazen

daven (Yid.)—to pray

dinim—Jewish laws

einikel (Yid.)—grandchild

ezras nashim—women's section of a synagogue

frum (Yid.)—religiously observant

gut Shabbos (Yid.)—have a good Sabbath

hachnosas orchim—the mitzvah of inviting guests into one's home

halacha—Jewish law

Hamalach Hagoel—(lit., the angel who protects); The Biblical blessing of Jacob to his grandsons which is recited in the Shema

hamotzi—blessing made over bread

Hashem ya'azor—G-d will help

kepele (Yid.)—head

klutz (ed)—lounge around and do nothing

kneidel (Yid.)—matza ball

kosher—halachic dietary regulations

Krias Shema—The recitation of the Shema

krechtz (Yid.)—sigh or moan

kumzits (Yid.)—(lit., come sit); an expression referring to a group sitting and singing heartfelt songs

lebedig (Yid.)—lively

loshon hora—(lit., the evil tongue); gossip

mabul—the great flood that took place in the times of Noach

Maoz Tzur—A song customarily sung after lighting the Chanukah candles

mein kindt (Yid.)—my child

mentch (Yid.)—(lit., a man); but can be used for both males and females to refer to someone well-refined with good character traits

mezuzah—(lit., doorpost); a small parchment with the Shema and two other Biblical passages inscribed on it. It is affixed to each doorpost in a Jewish home as a reminder of G-d's oneness and our moral duties to Him.

midos tovos—good character traits

Modeh Ani—(lit., I thank you); the first prayer said upon awakening each morning

morah—teacher

Motzei Shabbos—Saturday night

nebach, neb, nebbish (Yid.)—a pity

negel vasser (Yid.)—(lit., water for the nails); the ritual washing of the hands first thing in the morning

netilas yedayim—washing of the hands; referring to the ritual washing of hands before eating bread

oy, vey (Yid.)—oh, no

parsha—(lit., section); figuratively, means the whole story; practically it usually refers to a section of the Torah

pshat—explanantion

Rashi—biblical commentator

rebbe—rabbi, teacher

Ribono Shel Olam—Master of the World

ruach—spirit

seder—order

seforim—books

Shabbos—the Sabbath

shaitel (Yid.)—wig

shepping nachas (Yid.)—receiving pleasure

shiva—the seven days of mourning after a close relative passes away

shlumpy—untidy; messy

shmoozed, shmoozing (Yid.)—talked

siddur—prayer book

simcha—celebration

tante (Yid.)—aunt

tefillah, tefillos—prayer(s)

Tehillim—book of Psalms

tzaddikim—holy, pious men

tzedakah—money for the poor and needy

vus iz dus (Yid.)—what is this?

Yom Tov, Yomim Tovim—holiday, holidays

zemiros—songs or hymns sung on Shabbos and holidays

zichrona l'vracha—may her memory be blessed